The Quest of the Land of the Eagle Feathers

The Book of Fall

I0545259

By

Joe G. Morin & Jo Ann Bullard

Copyright© 2019

Published by

Lyrics and Books from the Heart

Publishing Company, Inc.

Preface

Don't walk behind me; I may not lead. Don't walk in front of me, I may not follow. Walk beside me that we can be as one.
Native American Proverb

The Keepers of the Yawi are on a quest to find the third book of the series of four: *The Book of Fall.* They have found *The Book of Spring* and *The Book of Summer.* They must find *The Book of Fall* in order to find the clues to where the last and most important book, *The Book of Winter,* is located. If they don't, The Land of the Eagle Feathers will not survive.

There has been a disaster of unknown nature in The Land of the Eagle Feathers. Nobody knows if The Land of the Eagle Feathers survived. Two of the main characters, Moses and One Feather are missing in the land. The Keepers of the Yawi must wait until the proper time to enter the land to look for the answers.

It is an agonizing time for the group. Their emotions are overwhelming. Time never went so slow. They must hope for the best. They must prepare for the worst. They must find out if their companions and the land survived.

There will be challenges, deceptions, trials and tribulations in this quest. Secrets will be revealed. Their enemies will be more dangerous, but not as dangerous as their own demons.

- Will The Land of the Eagle Feathers survive?
- Will Moses and One Feather be found alive?
- Will they defeat their own demons?
- Will they find The Book of Fall?
- Will everyone survive?

Table of Contents

Chapter I

What do they do now?

The dust in the tunnel slowly fell to the tunnel's floor. The group looked out of the tunnel at **The Land of the Eagle Feathers** in sheer horror. They were all in shock. In front of them was a wasteland of boulders, uprooted trees, burned grass and deep cuts in the land. Nothing seemed to have been spared. What once was a beautiful grassy field of lush grass and wildflowers had been total destroyed.

It looked more like a moonscape. It was barren of any life. Fire from beneath the ground flared up in the crevices that were open and crisscrossed the land before them. What was once a dense green forest about a mile away was now reduced to a big pile of wooden trunks lying on the ground like matchsticks. How anyone could have survived this was very unlikely.

Suddenly, the mountain started to shake. Rocks and large boulders started to fall from the mountain above. The tunnel started to cave in around them. Everyone ran. As the last one jumped out of the tunnel, several large boulders sealed the tunnel shut.

Dust covered everyone. As the dust settled, a smoky haze covered the sky. It was difficult to see the distant mountains. As the group gathered at the bottom of the small hill in front of the tunnel, dark clouds started to form. Everyone was worried about what could have happened to Moses, One Feather and Angela. Were they still alive? They could only hope. They had come back to **The Land of the Eagle Feathers** to try to save them, besides wanting to find the third book of *The Land of the Eagle Feathers: The Book of Fall.*

Dark clouds filled the sky. Lightning flew between the thunderheads. Some of the clouds started to move to form shapes. It wasn't long before a shape of a head of a dark brown and black wolf formed. It seemed to cover the sky ahead of them. The wolf, looking directly at them, spoke, "We have been expecting you. You can see what destruction you have caused to this sacred land by taking *The Book of Summer* from this land. Even though, you had been warned about doing so. The Great Spirits are angry."

June looked at the wolf, "I know you think that we are not worthy because we have faults. You do not trust us. You feel that we will take the books and use them selfishly. The power that the last book, *The Book of Winter,* contains is what you fear. With that book, we could obtain anything we would ever want. I can only speak for myself. I would only use that power to protect this land. The Great Spirits cannot protect this land. They must use humans to protect it from harm. The destruction we see before us is a warning from you to show what the power of *The Book of Winter* can do."

The wolf replied, "What you say is true. We do not trust you. This sacred land is in danger of being taken from The Council of Elders by evil beings. We cannot intervene in this struggle. The powers of the Council are weakening by each passing moment. They have been weakened by using their powers over centuries to keep out beings that would exploit this sacred land.

John has stated that you can find the last two books of **The Land of the Eagle Feathers.** You must first find *The Book of Fall*. It will not be easy. We are not so sure. Finding the next two books will not be an easy task. Nobody has ever gotten close to finding them. We will watch but will not help you."

Everyone turned to look at me. I looked at the wolf, "I have given you many years of my life to protect this land. I will save this land, or I will destroy it. I will finish my journey here. It is that simple. Evil will not be allowed to have the powers that this land possesses. We cannot allow anyone to obtain the

5

other two books. If they do so, they will be able to conquer this land. Many of us fear that they will have the power to conquer our world as well. We will not become slaves to them. Evil must not be allowed to triumph."

The wolf looked at me. "We know what you say is true. John, you have changed through the years. We do not know if your heart is true. Can you keep this group of yours, **The Keepers of the Yawi,** under control? Not all of them can be trusted. We will see. Power has a way of corrupting humans."

The wolf's eyes were like fire, **"We know that you will be searching for the other members of your group. You should know that they probably have only a few more days to live. They are in bad shape. You must find them, or they will die. You have many tests in front of you. John, use your powers wisely."** The wolf's face faded into the dark storm clouds. Loud claps of thunder followed with a torrent of rain starting to fall.

Everyone put on their rain jackets. We were at a lost as to where to start looking for Moses, One Feather and Angela. There was an outcropping by the tunnel. I had the group get under it to discuss what to do next. We settled down to discuss our next move. Lo Ming spoke first, "I know Moses. He would try to make it to the sacred mountain. He would know that we would have to come there." Antonio agreed with her. "That is where I would go. I would think that the sacred mountain would be spared from this destruction." Everyone nodded in agreement.

That left One Feather and Angela. I spoke next, "One Feather would probably go to the sacred mountain also. I do not think that Angela would do the same." Antonio, Angela's lover, asked me, "Why?" I hesitated to answer him. Antonio was starting to get angry. He knew that I had not told him everything about what I knew about Angela. It didn't take long for everyone to look at me for answers about why Angela could enter **The Land of the Eagle Feathers.** It had become apparent to them I knew more. "I can only tell you that Angela must tell you, not me. You must hear it from her. I can tell you that Angela and I were once enemies. In fact, she tried to kill me several times. We have a truce now. I promised her that I would not tell anyone about our past. She helped save me. I only know that I must save her. It is the law of this land."

Nick started to say something, but Rose stopped him. She did not want anyone to know about Zan. Zan had been her love many years ago. His father had banished him to somewhere in **The Land of the Eagle Feathers**. She thought it best that nobody else knew about him. It would only complicate matters more.

Mary finally spoke up, "All this talk is getting us nowhere. We need to get started. While all of you were talking, I took my field glasses and started looking at the edge of the forest about a mile from here. There appears to be some sort of sign there. I think I saw an arrow with a necklace or bracelet attached to it. It was a bright shiny stone that attracted me to that area. I don't know about you, but I think that is where we should start looking."

The rain had stopped. Mary had gotten up. I grabbed her by her wrist. "We will let June and her wolf lead us to that spot. We must be very careful. A wrong step could be the last one. Her wolf would be best able to find a way through all this destruction." Mary pointed toward where she saw the sign. June clapped her hands and her black wolf, Midnight, appeared. She whispered in Midnight's ear. Midnight slowly started toward the woods at the edge of what was once a great forest. It now lay in ruins. The mighty Oak trees had been tossed around like sticks in an old game called "Pick up Sticks."

It had taken us several hours to go halfway across the field toward the forest. Several times, Midnight had to double back to keep from falling into hidden crevices in the soft ground. Antonio had to grab Lo Ming once before she would have fallen into a fiery pit of lava. At the rate of speed, we were going, it would be nightfall when we would be able to get to the area that Mary thought she saw the sign.

We all jumped when we heard the sound of dynamite exploding. We stopped and turned to look back. Someone had blown open the tunnel. We had to dodge some of the rocks that had been blown our way. Nick asked, "I wonder who could have blown open the tunnel for us." Nobody answered him. We were just grateful to see it open.

The old man and his dog looked out of the tunnel. "Don't worry. They can't see us. I only hope that they find what they are looking for. If they make it back here, they will be lucky to survive what is waiting for them. Didn't you see all the people coming up the trail behind us?" The old man's dog barked. "Yes, I know. Our friends will need some help by the way those troops look. I think we can give their enemies a few surprises. I only hope that it will be enough for John and the others to survive."

Midnight started howling. June knew why. She must have picked up the scent of Snow, One Feather's male wolf. Midnight and Snow were mates. June instinctively grabbed Midnight's neck. She would have to calm Midnight down. It would be Midnight's instinct to run to find Snow. June spoke to Midnight, "I am sorry. I have to do this for your sake." She clapped her hands, and Midnight disappeared. Nick saw this and took June by the hand. "I will find the rest of the way across this field. I have made it across many minefields in Iraq and other places. Just stay behind me and step where I step."

The Great Elder called a meeting with the Red Woman. The Red Woman arrived at the Council Room in the Cave just before dawn. She had a worried look on her face. She knew that the rest of the Council had been having second thoughts about what had been happening to **The Land of the Eagle Feathers**. The earthquakes had taken a toll on the land. Nobody in the tribes that inhabited **The Land of the Eagle Feathers** had been hurt. Rumors had been spreading that it was an omen that the land was in danger from the evil. It was up to the Great Elder and her to quiet these rumors.

The Great Elder was seated in the middle of the room by the large granite council table. This didn't surprise her. It was the man dressed in white buckskin with a long white Elk cape that did. His long white hair contrasted with his red leathery skin. He had a white gold band around his forehead with precious stones. His long Oak Staff with a white crystal on its end leaned against the table by him. He was seated directly opposite The Great Elder. Red Woman had only seen him a couple of times in her life. His name was White Elk. He was the most powerful shaman in **The Land of the Eagle Feathers**. He was old and wise beyond anyone's years. To have him here meant something very important was happening. He only showed himself when very dire and dangerous events were coming.

The Great Elder pointed to a seat between the two in the middle of the table. Red Woman nodded toward White Elk and The Great Elder to show her respect. Then she seated herself. White Elk rose from his seat to speak. "I have come to speak to you. The earthquakes are a symbol of things that are happening to this land. It appears that the prophesies have come true. The two wolves have been fighting."

The Great Elder replied, "Yes, they have. The good and bad spirits are fighting for control of this land and ourselves."

9

"You know that everyone has those two spirits or wolves within themselves. It had been said that when the second book, *The Book of Summer*, would be found that there would be a price to pay. The wolves would fight for dominance. Good would fight evil. This time we are grateful that the good wolf won. The destruction of our land has stopped for now," stated White Elk.

The Great Elder spoke, "We have no choice but to find the other books. We have become too weak to keep evil out of this land. We know that the closer **The Keepers of the Yawi** get to the last book the more that we and everyone here will have to face their demons."

"I fear that you have unleashed both the good and bad within us. Getting those books can save this land, but at what cost. The people that are trying to get the books are not pure in heart. They have demons within themselves. Will they save us, or will they destroy us? I have come to tell you that when the winter season is over: either **The Land of the Eagle Feathers will survive**, or it will be taken over by the evil ones. Our time is running out.

I only hope that you and Red Woman are being guided by the White wolf and not the Black wolf. I sense that one of your Council is not. Night Panther has reasons of his own to try to stop, **The Keepers of the Yawi**. I only know that events will be happening that are out of our control."

"What you said is true. We have only two choices in our lives; to follow good or to follow bad. This sacred land is about the only good that is left. To allow it to fall like so many others would be the end of all that is good. Evil has a way of winning, but so does good. We can only hope that there is enough good in **The Keepers of the Yawi** to save us. May we all survive. May good triumph, and evil be defeated," the Red Woman said with a heavy heart.

White Elk started to leave. He turned one last time to speak. "The land is starting to feel the battle to come. Spirits are unsettled. Time is short. Evil is starting to penetrate this land. The Evil Red Bear and two of his men have already made it into the land. They were too powerful for our defenses to stop them. They are tracking some of John's people. Angela is trying to save them. Let's hope that she is listening to the White Wolf. You know what she did before. She is not pure of heart. May the spirits protect us." White Elk didn't wait for anyone to reply. He just disappeared.

Nick took out two sections of tent poles from his pack. He put them together. He then tied his K-Bar military knife to the end of them. He would use this to probe the ground ahead of him for any weakness. It was very slow going. Each step Nick made, everyone behind him followed in his footsteps. Twice Nick had to change direction when his knife cut too easily into the ground. Finally, they reached the end of the field. Here the ground was hard and safe.

A doe and her fawn ran into the field. The fawn disappeared into a crevice that had formed. The mother deer stopped and looked down. Nick stopped everyone. "It is our fault that the little deer ran. We scared it. It is our responsibility to save it," he stated.

June spoke to the doe in her native language. The doe moved back into the broken forest. Antonio attached a rope from his pack to Nick. Everyone took hold of the rope and let Nick start toward the crevice where the fawn had fallen into. Nick slowly inched his way there. He looked down and saw that the fawn was not hurt.

The fawn was about 10 feet down. He told everyone to give him about 10 feet of slack. He was going to jump down and tie his rope to the fawn. June went over to the crevice and talked to the fawn. What she saw scared her. Lava was starting to

11

spill into the crevice. She didn't know if Nick had time to save the fawn and himself. She tried to talk Nick out of it, but he insisted on trying to save the fawn. Nick jumped into the crevice. Quickly, he tied his rope to the fawn. June gave the signal for everyone to pull the fawn out. As fast as they could, they pulled. When they had the fawn out, June untied it and whispered in its ear to go to his mother. Then she tossed the rope to Nick. The lava was almost to Nick. Nick started to climb as June had everyone pull as hard as they could. As Nick topped the top of the crevice, the lava shot straight out of the crevice. June pulled Nick toward the others. She heard Nick groan. Some lava had gotten on Nick's thigh. She took her knife and cut his pants and pulled them off. Luckily, Nick's leg was only badly burned. It could have been much worse.

Mary got out her medicine bag and started to attend to Nick's leg. She was going to give him some drugs for the pain. Nick stopped her. He was not going to go down that road again. "I will just have to deal with it. I am not going to have any more drugs in my system," he yelled. Rose ran over and took out some potion she had. This is not a drug. It will stop the pain a little. She took out a red stone and moved it near the bad burn. Nick jumped then settled down. He passed out. Rose looked at Mary, "Don't worry! His pain will be gone when he wakes up. I put it into the red stone. He will need attending to for the next few weeks."

Lo Ming and June had ran over to the arrow and bracelet. On the arrow was some dried blood. The bracelet was the one that Lo Ming had given Moses the night before she pushed him out of the tunnel. Both Lo Ming and June were beside themselves with worry. "They can handle themselves; they have someone helping them," I said. "What do you mean?" ask Lo Ming. Antonio pointed out a woman's footprint. "Angela is taking care of them," I would recognize her boot print anywhere. She gets a special kind of boot that leaves this mark."

June looked at the tracks closely. She saw what I saw. There were some other footprints. These were from Indian moccasins. There were three sets. One had the sign of a snake on it. It was only a day or two old. June said, "Somehow Red Bear is here. He and two warriors are tracking them. They want to kill One Feather and Moses. I had a fight with him this summer. He will stop at nothing to stop us. We need to find One Feather, Moses and Angela before they do." I told her that we cannot do anything tonight. We need to pitch camp and rest. We need light to track them. We will start after them at first light." Antonio agreed. "I pity them when they meet Angela."

It didn't take long for the group to pitch their camp for the night. Lo Ming noticed a small tree with leaves that were beginning to turn colors. It seemed a little early for that to happen. She guessed that it had something to do with the altitude or the environment caused by the earthquakes. Even though Nick was hurt, he insisted on fixing the evening meal on the campfire. He made a stew of jerky and dried vegetables. He told everyone that making supper helped keep his mind off two things: the pain of his burns and Shanna.

After their meal, the group sat around the campfire. Nobody was in the mood to get some sleep. Everyone was worried about what was happening to One Feather, Moses and Angela. Lo Ming tried to take everyone's mind off this by asking June to tell her the legend of why leaves change their color in fall. June, being Native American, could not help herself but to tell everyone the legend.

June stood up in front of the group, "I will tell you about this, but I don't know if it's a myth or true. This has been passed down by all great medicine men and women in my tribe for many centuries." With the fire behind her, she began her story. She also used sign language as she told it. She thought that they might learn some sign by listening to her when she spoke.

"The legend of the Leaves:
Why Fall has leaves of many colors?"

+ There is a legend of why the trees turn many colors in the fall. Many moons ago and circles of the sun, there was a Great Bear. The Great Bear had his own large territory on earth. A Great Deer thought that the Great Bear was selfish because he had claimed so much territory. The Great Deer wanted just as much territory. The only territory that was left to claim was in the Skyland across the Rainbow Bridge. The Rainbow Bridge was the only way to get to the Skyland, which to the animals was like heaven.

The Great Deer was angry and decided to go to claim part of the Skyland for himself. The Great Deer thought if he went in the Season called Fall everyone would be too busy getting ready for Winter to see him cross the Rainbow Bridge. This was not to be.

The Great Bear happened to look up. He saw the Great Deer cross the Rainbow Bridge to the Skyland. That was too much for the Great Bear. He ran after the Great Deer. The Great Bear crossed the Rainbow Bridge and confronted the Great Deer.

"Why are you here in the Skyland." the Great Bear said to the Great Deer.

"I am here because I wanted more territory like you have, and none is left," said the Great Deer.

"You must leave the Skyland and go back to earth," said the Great Bear.

The Great Deer argued with the Great Bear that he could not make the Great Deer go back. The only one that could make the Great Deer to do that was the Great Wolf.

"You are not the Great Wolf. You cannot make me go back. You are overstepping your position in the Animal Council. I will not go back," said the Great Deer.

The Great Bear had enough from the Great Deer. Soon they were in a great battle with each other. Lightning flashed, and thunder echoed down from the Skyland as they fought each other. This attracted some of the other animals of the Animal Council. They saw what was happening and sent for the Great Wolf to stop the fight.

When the Great Wolf arrived, he went across the Rainbow Bridge to stop the fight. He stopped the fight, but it was too late to stop the Great Deer from hurting the Great Bear. One of the Great Deer's horns had cut the Great Bear badly. Blood covered both of the Great Deer's horns.

The Great Deer, seeing the Great Wolf, ran back down the Rainbow Bridge to earth. As the Great Deer ran from the sky, blood from his horns fell to earth landing on the great forests of earth turning their tree leaves many colors.

That is why in Fall the trees turn many colors. It is to celebrate that no animal can cross the Rainbow Bridge without permission from the Great Wolf and the Great Spirit.

As she finished as if on cue, a howl of a wolf could be heard in the distance. This added to the drama of the story. June smiled at the sound. It had to be Snow, One Feather's wolf. She knew that One Feather must still be alive. She wanted to clap her hands and let Midnight loose to run after Snow. I stopped June. "I know that you want to let Midnight out to go to Snow. You cannot do that. Red Bear may see Midnight and kill her. It would let Red Bear know we are here. We need to surprise Red Bear and his two followers to have a chance of defeating them.

If they know we are coming, they could set up an ambush for us. They could follow Midnight and find our people more easily. I don't think that Red Bear will be near here tonight, but I will take first watch. Nick can take the next. His wounds will keep him awake most of night. Lo Ming and Antonio will take the last watch. If anyone gets sleepy, have Rose or Mary take yours. Now get some sleep."

Everyone went to their tents. I took my seat just outside of the fire's light. The night was warm. If anyone was near, they would be attracted by the campfire. I liked looking at the stars. It reminded me of the night sky in the desert of the Southwest. Several years ago, I was guiding a young woman wanting to find some relics. One of the relics was a tablet that was supposed to be Mayan or Aztec. It would have the secrets of what were medicines that they used to cure many illnesses. We fell in love that summer. There were only a few times in my long life that I was happy. That summer was one of them. I tried only to remember the good times of that summer. It was too bad that it ended so tragically. At least, I had thought so until the Red Woman told me different. I didn't know what to think anymore. I did know that the Red Woman and I were going to have a long talk. She had kept some secrets. I would get the truth out of her.

Chapter II
Will they find them?

Rose woke me just before dawn. Nick had made breakfast. We ate in silence. There was a lot on each one of our minds. This journey of ours, especially the last few months, had taken a toll on each of us. We had more questions than answers. My only concern was to keep everyone alive. We had to locate our other members and stay alive at the same time. We could not lose anyone. It would take all of us to find and obtain the next sacred book. Time was running out for us and this land.

June took the lead. She clapped her hands, and Midnight appeared. Midnight licked June. June whispered into her wolf's ear. Midnight nodded her head as if she understood her. "I told Midnight that she must track our people, but to be careful. She is not to make any noise or run to Snow. She understood why. Now follow me and Midnight. We don't have time to waste."

I put Antonio at the end of our line of march. Since Red Bear was a medicine man, I put Rose right behind June. Rose's voodoo and knowledge of the mystical arts would be helpful if Red Bear tried to ambush June. I knew that Red Bear was very jealous of June's skill as a Medicine Woman. He would try to kill her if he could. I put myself right behind Rose. Nick would be behind me. Mary and Lo Ming would look after him.

The further we got into the destroyed forest, the less the destruction was. After about three miles, the forest returned to normal. We were pleased that the destruction didn't destroy all the land. We stopped for a short break near a mountain stream. We filled our canteens and took a rest. Nick was holding up well considering his wounds. Lo Ming was worried about him.

Rose took out her small crystal ball. She was studying it. She was starting to piece together what had happened to our lost members. She told us that Moses and One Feather had been seriously hurt by the earthquake. One Feather had a broken arm and Moses had something happen to his right leg. It appeared that Angela had found them. She had been trying to go back to the tunnel when the earthquake hit. She had used some of her spare clothing to make bandages for their cuts and broken limbs. They had stayed at this stream several days until One Feather and Moses could travel. Rose couldn't get any more information from her crystal ball.

Throughout the years, I had gained many skills in mystical ways and magic. I never let anyone know that I had those that craft. I was keeping this a secret. This would give me an advantage if I had to use it. I was saving this for one man.

I got up and told everyone to move as fast as they could. Midnight was on the scent of her mate, Snow. John told everyone that there would be no more rest periods. It was now a race to catch up the Red Bear's group before they caught up to Angela's.

After two hours, Nick's wounds were beginning to slow him down. He was having more trouble walking. His right leg was swelling. Lo Ming located a small patch of trees that would provide him shelter off the main trail. Mary volunteered to stay with Nick and use her medical skills on him. She was afraid that he was starting to have an infection. His temperature was high. He had a fever. John told Mary to be very careful. Red Bear's group might come back this way. Mary told everyone they would hide in the patch of small trees until someone came back for them or Nick got better. Mary had her bow and arrows that would provide her some protection. Rose gave her some of her exploding beads. Mary told us to run. She would take care of Nick.

Red Bear was pleased with the progress his group was making. He figured that he was only a few hours away from finding part of John's group. He couldn't understand why they had been left behind. He had heard of the legend that one of **The Keepers of the Yawi** had to be left in **The Land of the Eagle Feathers** after *The Book of Summer* was found and taken out of the land. What he couldn't understand was why there were three people ahead of him? It didn't matter. He was a strong medicine man. He could take care of any three people. The only one that he worried about was June. She proved to be a great medicine woman. She just might have enough power to

18

defeat him. She was not supposed to be here in this land for another couple of weeks. He would make her suffer. He knew about One Feather, June's love. When he killed him, she would suffer. The arrow that was left at the end of the field was One Feather's. Red Bear could read the symbols on its shaft. He did not know who the bracelet belonged to. He knew by the signs left on the trail. At least two of the three were injured. He wondered who the woman was with them. He could tell by the footprints that one was a woman.

Angela was helping Moses climb a small hill. One Feather had Snow by his side. Snow started to growl at the trail behind them. Angela looked back. She could see several miles down the trail. One Feather saw movement. Looking very carefully, One Feather saw three men moving slowly up the trail toward them. Angela spotted them. She knew who one of them was right away. Only one person dressed in red buckskins with a white circle on his chest. This had to be Red Bear. One Feather recognized Red Bear also. Everyone ducked down behind some brush. Angela told One Feather and Moses that Red Bear would kill all of them. He was a man that wanted to stop anyone from getting the sacred books. He had wanted to destroy **The Land of the Eagle Feathers** ever since he had been banished from this land. Rumors were that he had been working for an evil group to take over the land.

One Feather told Angela and Moses that he would split up with them. He knew that Red Bear would want him because of his relationship with June. One Feather would leave signs for Red Bear to track him. Red Bear would let his other two men track down Angela and Moses. Angela didn't like One Feather's plan. She knew that One Feather could not defeat Red Bear. He was too powerful for anyone of them to fight. One Feather told her not to worry, He would try to find the only medicine man that could defeat Red Bear. He was located not too far from here. Angela knew who he meant. That medicine man was probably a myth. His name was White Elk. Only a few ever claimed to have seen him.

"How will you find White Elk?" Angela asked One Feather. One Feather was surprised that Angela knew who he was talking about. She must know more than she should. One Feather had felt something about her. Angela felt it too. They had a connection of some sort. When she had touched his arm to put it into a sling, her touch was soft. He had felt that touch before. Before Angela could say anything more, One Feather jumped up and ran away from them. He dropped an arrow on purpose for Red Bear to find on the trail behind him.

Angela grabbed Moses and pulled him up the hill. Moses was too weak to fight anyone. She had to find a place for them to hide. Maybe, those men would give up looking for them. Their only hope would be if John's group would have come back to find them. If they were on their way, June and Rose would be with them. They would be able to use their magical skills to save them.

Angela remembered there was a special place near here. She had played there when she was a child. If it was still there, they could hide there for several days before being found. She led Moses off the trail several hundred yards from the main trail. Angela went back and dusted off the trail so that their footprints would not be detected. Then she went back to Moses. Moses was not doing well. He had the Red Fever. People could get this fever if they were injured. Moses would come and go in this fever. He didn't know what he was doing sometimes. Angela knew that the Red Woman was the only one that could help him to survive. She had hoped to get him to her before Moses got worse.

There was a waterfall near about a half mile away. If she could get Moses there, he would be safe. Behind the waterfall was a cave. She could hide him there. Then she would go and try to find the Red Woman. It was Moses' only hope. The Red Woman had a cure for the fever that Moses had. It wasn't long before she got Moses to the waterfall. She led him behind the waterfall to the hidden cave. She told Moses to stay there. Moses nodded to her. She made him a bed of dried leaves and covered him with her jacket to keep him warm. She smiled at him and said, "I will bring you help and save you. If I don't, Lo Ming will be very upset with me." Moses laughed softly and lost consciousness. Angela knew time was short for Moses. She must hurry. She started to run for Eagle Mountain.

John and his group had made good time following the trail. It was easy to follow. Apparently Red Bear and his two followers did not expect anyone to be following them. They did not try to hide their tracks. John guessed that Red Bear was only a few hours ahead of them. John pressed everyone harder to make better time.

Red Bear was confused when he got to where Angela and One Feather split. He found the arrow by the trail that One Feather had taken. The woman's and the other man's footprints seem to have disappeared.

Red Bear didn't like what he had found. One Feather must had seen them coming up the trail behind them. Red Bear reasoned that One Feather must have taken off to lead him away from the others. One Feather was too smart to drop an arrow on the trail. Red Bear knew that One Feather was no match for him. It would only be a matter time before he located One Feather and killed him. He wondered if he should leave his two followers behind to try to find the other two or take them with him. Red Bear decided to take them with him. After all, One Feather was the most important target. Red Bear pointed to the two followers to follow him.

Angela knew these woods like the back of her hand. She took short-cuts through various parts of the forest. She had been on the run for two hours. Her lungs and legs were starting to ache. She had to stop for a few minutes. She hoped that the Red Woman would be easy to find. She knew many years ago the Red Woman would go to the warm springs to bathe and wash her clothes. She would have to take a chance and try there first. To climb up Eagle Mountain would take too long. The only other way to communicate with the Red Woman would be to use smoke. That would be dangerous for her because it would give away her location to Red Bear and the Great Elder. The Great Elder had warned her to never come to **The Land of the Eagle Feathers** again.

One Feather was running as fast as the swiftest deer. His wounds had mostly healed, but they had taken a toll on his stamina. He knew that he must find White Elk before Red Bear found him. One Feather had traveled about three miles to the far side of the Green Forest. The trail he was on ended at a steep cliff. One Feather saw paintings on the side of the cliff in front of him. One picture was of a Great White Elk. One Feather knew he was at the right place. The only problem was how was he going to contact White Elk before Red Bear and his followers found him.

June looked at the footprints on the trail. It looked like Red Bear and his followers were going after One Feather. Snow's paw prints were going the same way as the rest of the footprints. John and June figured that Red Bear was only about 30 minutes ahead of them. June clapped for Midnight to disappear. She didn't want her wolf to get hurt. She was afraid that Red Bear might try to kill Midnight if he got the chance. John decided to leave Antonio and Lo Ming on the hillside trail. He knew that Angela was probably close by with Moses. That would be the only reason they would have split up. Moses must be hurt seriously, or they would have stayed together.

John was worried that Lo Ming was being too distracted by what was happening to Moses. He knew that Lo Ming was worried about their relationship. Antonio and Lo Ming understood the need to find Angela and Moses. Antonio knew how Angela thought. He would figure where they might be. There had to be tracks somewhere near the side of this hill. He would find them.

June, John and Rose ran down the trail. They knew that they had to be careful. Red Bear may have seen them and could be setting up an ambush for them. John had told Rose that she and June were to take out Red Bears' followers. John would handle Red Bear. June told John that she should do that. John laughed and said, "You don't know me as well as you think."

Angela was about to the warm springs. She could only hope that the Red Woman was there. As she rounded a large boulder in the trail, she saw the steam from the hot springs. Slowly, she approached the hot spring. In the mist of steam, she could see an outline of a woman. Softly, Angela called out for the Red Woman. The mist in front of her parted. The Red Woman was standing in the middle of the hot spring. She was washing her clothes. The only clothes the Red Woman had on was a light linen dress.

The Red Woman yelled at Angela, "What are you doing here? You know the rules. You were banished from our tribe long ago." Angela replied, "Yes, I was, but you owe me one favor. I saved your life once. I now need you to save another. I am calling in that favor. You have no choice but to fulfill that favor. Then you will be free from me."

"What is the favor?" the Red Woman growled back at Angela.

"I need you to cure Moses of the Red Fever. He is dying in the cave by the waterfalls that I use to play in. We must hurry or he will die."

"I will grant you this favor because we must keep Moses alive to help save this land. You surprise me with your request. You may have changed from the one I knew long ago. Let me grab my bag of medicine by the edge of the boulder. We must run like the wind to be in time," commanded the Red Woman.

Antonio and Lo Ming searched the side of the hillside slowly. He knew that Angela had tried to hide her tracks. She would cover them for several hundred feet from the main trail. He decided to start looking for her sign about seven hundred feet for the main trail. They went due North from the trail. They saw a small stream in the bottom of the hill. It would be hard for Angela to hide her tracks completely there. They would follow the stream bank until they saw some little sign of her footprint or Moses' footprint. It took some very close and tedious work. Antonio finally noticed a bend in several leaves of a large plant that covered both sides of the small stream. Most people wouldn't have noticed the very slight bend in those leaves. He turned over the green leaves and saw a faint man's footprint. This is where I would have crossed the stream. The big leaves of the plant covered both sides of the stream. Angela was very good at concealing her trail.

Antonio took his time in following the very faint trail that Angela and Moses had left. Lo Ming was impressed with Antonio's tracking skill. She would have to ask him sometime where he learned to track. They had gone about a mile from the main trail when they saw a waterfall in a mountain stream. This was a large waterfall that fell at least 15 feet from the top to a pool of water at the bottom of the fall. Antonio noticed that it was wider than he thought it should be.

Antonio remembered that he had once hidden many years ago behind a waterfall like this one. It had been in the Northeast part of the United States. He had been running from some Huron Indians. They didn't like the side he was on. He was too tired to run much further when he saw a waterfall to his right. The Indians would be on him in a few minutes. He had decided to take a chance and hide behind the waterfall. He swam across the pool and dove under the falling water. When he came up for air, he discovered that he was in a small cave. The Indians could not see him. When they arrived at the scene, they thought he had run down the trail. The waterfall had saved his life. Maybe this waterfall will save Moses. Antonio pointed to the waterfall. He told Lo Ming that they would find Moses there behind the waterfall.

One Feather knew he was running out of time. Red Bear and his men would be here in a few minutes. One Feather looked at the cliff paintings to see if there was a clue to how to contact White Elk. One painting was of the man using a blanket to send smoke signals. The smoke in the painting was white. Could this be a clue on how to get White Elk's attention?

He didn't wait to think about it. He put some dry grass and small twigs in a pile. Taking his flint and using a piece of steel from his medicine bag, he sparked a small fire. He cut a green branch that was covered with large leaves. As the fire became bigger, he put the branch on the fire to make smoke. The smoke was not the right color. He needed white smoke. He looked at the paintings again. One painting showed a man throwing something on the fire in front of him. One Feather saw what he needed. At the base of the cliff was a white powder. He took a handful of the powder and threw it on the fire. The smoke of the fire turned white. Using the branch like a blanket, One Feather raised and lowered it to give up puffs of white smoke. He watched as the puffs of smoke rose toward the top of the tall cliff.

"That won't do you any good, One Feather," a low voice behind him said. One Feather turned toward the voice. He knew who it was. Standing there with his two followers was Red Bear. "Who do you think would be coming to help you, One Feather," Red Bear said to him. One Feather knew he was probably going to die. He would try to fight them, but it would probably be no use. They had magical powers besides having him outnumbered. He did have one trick up his sleeve.

As Red Bear and his followers got closer, they heard a howl behind them. A large white wolf appeared. One Feather took his large branch and shoveled some of the hot coals into the faces of the men in front of him. This blinded Red Bear and his men for a few seconds. The white wolf and One Feather jumped on the three men knocking them down. They seemed to get the better of the three men. Red Bear was able to get to his feet while the white wolf and One Feather were fighting his two followers. The next thing One Feather knew he was being tied to a tree. Red Bear had used his powers to overcome both of them.

One Feather looked for his white wolf but could not see him. "Don't worry about your white wolf. He ran away when I told him that I would kill you if he stayed. He is a smart wolf," stated Red Bear. One Feather could not move. Some sort of force besides the rope held him to the tree trunk. "Poor little June. She will be completely torn apart with grief over your death. I will let one of my followers kill you while I watch you die. It will be a slow painful death. I will enjoy it as much as my followers will. Now, he will start to make small cuts in your chest. Blood will flow very slowly. Then we will make more and more cuts. Each cut will be a little deeper and more painful. Go ahead and make your first cuts," commanded Red Bear to one of his followers.

One Feather showed no sign of distress when he was cut. Red Bear was impressed with One Feather's bravery. He ordered the man to cut deeper. Red Bear could see that One Feather did feel that cut. One Feather was starting to bleed more. Blood covered his chest. "In about an hour with a few more cuts, you will start dying. Too bad, you are a brave man. It is a waste for you to die like this," said Red Bear with respect.

I told June to get Midnight. "We need Midnight to reach One Feather. Maybe she and Snow can distract Red Bear. They must have caught up with One Feather by now. It will take us a few minutes to get there to help him," I told her. June clapped her hands, and Midnight appeared. "Go find Snow and One Feather and help them," she told Midnight. Midnight ran and howled as she did. There were several howls echoing through the forest. One was Snow, but the others were different.

One Feather was in bad shape. He was getting light-headed. Red Bear said, "It won't be long now. One more deep cut, and you will be finished, One Feather." As the man reached up to cut One Feather, the forest became alive with howls of wolves. The howls were so loud that he stopped and turned to look back at the forest behind them. A chorus of howling wolves filled the forest. It sounded as if hundreds of wolves were coming in their direction.

One Feather's wolf, Snow, appeared in the forest. Red Bear said. "Don't worry, it is a trick to get us to stop." Then another wolf appeared coming along beside Snow. That wolf was black with red demon like fiery eyes. It growled. One Feather knew that it was Midnight. June and John must be near. In a few seconds, several other wolves appeared from the shadows of the forest. It was a whole pack. Snow had gone to get his pack of wolves. They had come to help him. They had blood in their eyes.

"Don't worry! Our magic will protect us. I can destroy all these wolves," yelled Red Bear to his two followers. "We will combine all our magical powers to defeat them." "I don't think so" said a woman's voice from the forest. Red Bear knew the woman's voice. Beads of sweat started forming on his forehead. It had to be June.

"What's the matter, Red Bear? You look like you just seen a ghost," said Rose as June and her walked out of the forest. "There are only two of you. There are three of us." Red Bear growled back in disrespect. "He will see a ghost. I am here," I said as I walked out of the forest behind them.

Red Bear saw me as I walked out of the forest. "I finally get to kill you, John," he said with a laugh. "I will take care of you personally, Red Bear. I have been waiting to teach you a lesson for a long time. You have always thought I knew nothing about mystic arts and magic. I will show you what I have learned all these many years. Don't worry, I won't kill you. I will let June do that some other time outside of **The Land of the Eagle Feathers**," laughing back at Red Bear.

"We will see," replied Red Bear as he pointed his staff and shot a bolt of lightning at me. I put up my right hand and caught it like a baseball. I made it into a ball and threw it back at Red Bear. The other men started fighting with June and Rose. The wolves made sure that nobody would escape from this fight.

Soon the mountainside was lit with fireworks from all the fighting taking place. June was doing fine with her attacker. She had knocked him down and was holding him in some sort of force field. Rose used some of her exploding beads. The beads had blown her man against the cliff and knocked him out. They both looked at my fight with Red Bear. He was good, but

I was better. I had lost my temper when I saw what he had done to One Feather. I was about to kill Red Bear when a flash of light blinded all of us." In the middle of the fight, White Elk appeared. "We will have none of that, John. I have been watching this fight, and you have won," said White Elk. With his staff, White Elk pointed it at the three men. Red Bear and his two followers disappeared into a puff of smoke. "I sent them back to where they came, out of this land. I see that I have taught you well, John," said White Elk. White Elk went over to One Feather. He cut One Feather down and laid his staff on One Feather's chest. A white glow of energy flowed into One Feather. One Feather's wounds healed in front of them. June ran to One Feather with tears running down her face. One Feather said, "What took you so long? I missed you." Both their wolves howled at them, and then they took off with the wolf pack into the forest.

It didn't take Antonio long to find a way in behind the waterfall. It was dark in the cave. He could hear a person groan in the far corner of the cave. It sounded like Moses. Antonio took out his flashlight and pointed it toward the sound. A man was covered with a jacket. Antonio recognized the jacket. It was Angela's jacket. Moses must be under it. He ran over and looked under the jacket. It was Moses. Antonio was startled by Moses' appearance. He looked like he was dying. Antonio knew that look. He had seen it in the sickness in Europe called the Black Plague years ago. Moses didn't have long to live.

Antonio heard noise behind him. "Get out of our way! We don't have much time to save Moses!" shouted Angela as the Red Woman pushed Antonio away. "Start a fire with some of the small sticks and twigs. I will make some of the sacred healing smoke to try to save him. I hope we are not too late," the Red Woman ordered. Antonio did as he was told. It wasn't long before he had a small fire going. The Red Woman had taken out of her medicine bag an eagle feather. She had made small symbols of animals and planets with colored sand on the dirt floor of the cave. She had Antonio and Angela move Moses close to the fire and symbols. The Red Woman poured some powders and put some plants on the small fire. Smoke of many colors rose from the fire. Taking her eagle feather, she slowly stroked the smoke over Moses' body. She whispered for Moses to breathe the smoke into his lungs. She sang and chanted many ancient songs over Moses while continuing to direct the smoke over Moses.

After the Red Woman left, Angela told Antonio she would have to go. Antonio didn't want her to and tried to persuade her to stay. Lo Ming was attending to Moses. Angela told him about what the Red Woman told her to do. She was to mention to Antonio the need to have June tell everyone about the Ghost Dance. It seems that the Council had decided to have this ceremony at the Council Meeting in a few days. There is a purpose for having the Ghost Dance.

The Red Woman stated that June and Antonio must keep careful watch over John. "All she said was something about the history of the Ghost Dance could be very disturbing to John. He was there. There was all she would say," said Angela. Antonio immediately understood what the Red Woman meant. It all fit together. John was one of those. He was much older than anyone thought. Antonio had thought about little things John had said to him. Things about history like he was there and not just telling about what he had read or heard. Yes, he knew people like John because he was one of them himself.

Angela gave Antonio a long passionate kiss. He held her tight. Angela said, "The Great Elder must never know I was here. You must promise me that. Tell the others to keep it quiet. My life depends on it." Angela went out the cave entrance. She said she would be going back to Houston. She had been gone too long.

Antonio went to check on Moses. Moses was breathing better. He had been sweating. His clothes were soaked. Antonio felt Moses's forehead. Antonio noted that Moses' fever had broken. Antonio was relieved. Antonio leaned over and whispered into Moses' ear. He told Moses that he must go and get the rest of the group. Moses must not move until he got back. Lo Ming nodded in agreement.

Moses hurried back to where John and the other had left him. From the hillside he could see the trail behind him. Something moved back down the trail. He had to be patient. It would be soon that he could see who was coming up the trail toward him.

Antonio was elated to discover that the two people walking slow toward him were Mary and Nick. He asked Mary how she cured Nick so fast. Mary said it was not that hard. She knew Native American medical cures. She had studied all native tribes in various cultures and countries. It appears that the native Indian cures worked the best in **The Land of the Eagle Feathers**. Antonio told them to have a seat. Antonio felt that the everyone else would be here in a few hours. He told them about Moses and the cave. They waited together until the rest of them arrived. It was starting to get dark.

 He led the way to the cave where Moses was. They were shocked to see the condition that Moses was in. Antonio told them that Moses was 100% better since the Red Woman had cured him. Lo Ming did not know how Moses would treat her. She would follow the advice that Moses' mother had told her to do. She hoped that it would work.

Mary and Nick volunteered to cook supper for everyone. Nick had lit a campfire in the cave. It gave the cave a warm feeling and light to see. It didn't take long to get everyone fed.

Moses took a little longer because he was too weak to feed himself.

When everyone was through eating, Antonio told everyone about the Red Woman and how she saved Moses. Antonio said that the Red Woman told him that the Council will be having a demonstration of the Ghost Dance to honor them. She wanted June to tell them some things about it so they could understand its meaning.

Antonio decided that he would not say anything to anyone about what Angela told him about John. He would watch John himself. Nobody but him should know John's past.

June had everyone set in a semi-circle. She felt honored to talk about the Ghost Dance and what it meant to the Indian people. This is a summary of what she told them.

The Ghost Dance

The Ghost Dance was started by a Paiute Medicine Man on the Great Plains in the 1880's named Wovoka. He was the son of a powerful Medicine Man. Wovoka had a vision during a solar eclipse. This vision was a group of Native Americans dancing in a circle in their encampment. He said that the purpose of the dance was to improve the life of the Indian people. People would dance in a circle for several days. As they danced, many people that had been killed in battle with the White man would appear next to them. The buffalo would return, and prosperity would return to the tribes. The white man would leave or vanish. Everything would be new and better for the tribes.

Wovoka thought he was the Messiah. He was to spread the word about the Ghost Dance to all tribes. It was said that when the Ghost Dance would start there might be only a few members of the tribe dancing. After several hours, there would be hundreds of members dancing. This was because the dead warriors were returning to help their people. These warriors could have bullet holes in them. A dance with a few people such as ten would become a dance of 500.

With Wovoka's assistance, the Ghost Dance spread throughout the Western United States including Canada and Mexico. This made the White man very concerned. White man had a way of taking something good and making it bad or destroying it. The white man began to try to stop the Ghost Dances. They were scared about the Indians, and what they might do. They rounded up tribal leaders. Many Indians were killed by them. That is another story. The Ghost Dance was the last final chance for the Indian race to become whole again. It had become very sacred to the Indians. No matter how much the white man tried, the Ghost Dance is remembered by most tribes. I will tell you more about the history of the Ghost Dance later.

It is getting late. We need to get some sleep. It has been a long day. Antonio says in a few days after Moses gets well, the Council will have a warrior to visit us to tell us to come to the Council meeting. Be very careful and treat the warrior with the utmost respect. He will be a famous warrior from the Ghost Dance days many years ago. The Council will honor us with a real Ghost Dance."

Antonio kept his eye on John. When June finished, John got up and walked out into the night. Antonio followed him. He could see that John was very disturbed about what June had told about the Ghost Dance. Antonio had heard about the Ghost Dance many years ago. He knew that John had been there. John had been scarred from what had happened on the plains so many years ago.

John sat down near the waterfall's pool. He just stared into it. Antonio could tell the memories so long ago that John had repressed in his mind were coming to life. Antonio was very worried about how John would take a real Ghost Dance. Antonio felt it was up to him to see that John would survive. He owed John that much.

Chapter III
What will happen in the Council Meeting?

After two days' rest, Moses and Nick were almost at full strength. They would be able to travel. They were eating breakfast when a flash of light blinded them in the cave. A man in full Indian dress of white buckskin covered with shining white crystals appeared. June recognized him at once. She had seen pictures of him in her studies of American Indians. June spoke to him, "Welcome, Wovoka! We are honored to have such a guest as you." Wovoka looked directly at John. In sign language, Wovoka spoke to John. John replied in kind. Wovoka nodded. He stood patiently in the middle of the cave. John told the others they must leave to follow Wovoka to the Council Meeting and the Ghost Dance.

It didn't take long for the group to gather their things. John told them it would take most of the day to arrive at the meeting place. They followed Wovoka. John was right behind Wovoka. Nobody said a word out of respect for Wovoka. At times, Wovoka seemed more spirit than man. Everyone knew it was a great honor to have such a great warrior and Shaman to escort them.

Wovoka escorted the group to a mountain ridge, overlooking a large meadow. The group wondered why this was so different from where they had been seated before. Wovoka explained that this Council Meeting would be different than the ones before. It was twilight. The twilight gave a mystical feel to the setting. Torches were lit all around the meadow.

Suddenly, the group heard a loud clap of thunder. The Great Elder and the Red Woman appeared. The Great Elder said,

"Welcome, my friends. We are ready to begin the Ghost Dance. We feel that is necessary to do this dance. Its purpose is to replenish the land and to remind you and ourselves of our purpose. Let us begin."

It was beginning to get dark. An eeriness filled the air as all became quiet. The sound of one lone drumbeat began to break the silence. Dancers appeared in their Ghost Dance outfits. Each outfit was decorated with pictures of the moon, sun and stars. The dancers joined hands and formed a circle. They moved to the side and then inward towards the center of the circle bending their knees and going backward and forward. Wovoka appeared in the center of the circle.

Another circle of dancers appeared, repeating the movements of the first circle. Circle after circle appeared. Each circle had an honored person in the middle beating a drum to the rhythm of the first circle. With each appearance of a new circle, the drumbeats got louder.

The meadow could not hold all the circles of the dancers. Circles of dancers appeared in the air above the dancers on the ground. One circle upon another circle until the sky was full of circles with hundreds, even thousands of dancers. The light of the Blood moon lit the sky giving a ghostly light to the sky and dancers.

As the circles rose into the sky, the group wondered where did all these dancers come from? They knew that one purpose of this dance was to reunite the Indians with their dead ancestors. The group was beginning to think that the Ghost Dance had fulfilled its purpose.

There was another loud clap of thunder. Another circle formed. June gasped when she saw Sitting Bull in the middle of the circle. You could see two bullet wounds in his body. One was in the chest, and the other was in the head. You could see bullet holes in the clothes of the other dancers in the circle.

Antonio was watching John closely. John appeared to handle the Ghost Dance well until he saw this circle. As the dancers' images became clear in this circle, John started trembling. John jumped up from his seat. He was looking at three dancers in this circle. There was a young woman and two children: a boy and young girl.

John could not hold back his emotions. His screaming cry of torment that he had held all these years came bubbling up from within him. Immediately, the dancers stopped. They looked at John and nodded. The young woman and her two children waved at John and disappeared. Slowly, one by one, the circles disappeared until the only one was the last one. Sitting Bull nodded at our group. Then the last circle started to disappear. John called to Sitting Bull. "Thank you," was all he said. Sitting Bull nodded. "Your family is safe as long as **The Land of the Eagle Feathers** is safe. That is why we came tonight. You know what you must do." Sitting Bull disappeared.

Antonio realized that John was starting to break down. He could feel he must get John calmed down before the Council Meeting. He grabbed John and told him to sit down. "John, you got to get it together. The Council Meeting will be starting soon. You must clear your head. There is too much riding on what is going to happen next."

For some reason, Mary came over to John. She had Antonio move to a different seat. She pulled John close to her. Putting her arms around him, she told him to let it all out. John pulled her tight to him. Tears were coming down his face. John was crying. All he kept saying was, "I loved them so much. I got there too late. I have never forgiven myself." Mary answered him back, "It wasn't your fault. You did all you could have. Many people lost loved ones that day. You still have the chance to save some of them."

John looked up at Mary, "How did you know?" I could tell by what Sitting Bull said and the look on your face. My mother had a book that she left me. I read her diary. There was a story about a White Man in it. I think that White Man was you."

June came over and whispered something in John's ear. After that, John seemed to calm down. John kissed Mary on her forehead and thanked her for helping him. He told everyone that he was now ready for the Council Meeting. He knew why they had the Ghost Dance.

Wovaka motioned for all of them to follow him. They all filed into a great cave. Torches were lit to give them light. There was a great table where all the Great Chiefs and Medicine men of the Council sat. John and his group were motioned to sit on a great oak log to face them. The Great Elder rose. "We are here at the Council Meeting to find out where John's heart lies. Only John can tell us that. I have the Talking Stick to give him. We must know. Remember, when you have the Talking Stick in your hands, you must tell the truth. You must tell us what your heart has in it." The Great Elder walked over to John. He had John stand. John stood up and took the Talking Stick.

John looked at all that were present. Then he began: I was a dispatch rider for the 7th Calvary in 1890, when all of the following happened. In 1890, the Ghost Dance swept through most of the tribes of the plains. Many white settlers and the army felt that this dance would cause an uprising of the Native Indians. Everything became very tense and political. The newspapers promoted this belief.

The Indian Commission and other political people wanted Sitting Bull to stop the practice of the Ghost Dance. Instead of stopping it, Sitting Bull promoted it. On December 15, 1890, James McLaughlin sent Indian police to arrest Sitting Bull for not stopping the Ghost Dances. During this incident, one of Sitting Bull's men, Catch the Bear, fired at Lt. Bull Head striking his right side. Lt. Bull Head turned and shot Sitting Bull, hitting him in his left side. Another police officer, Red Tomahawk, shot Sitting Bull in the head. Both men died from their wounds the next day.

On December 28, 1890, Spotted Elk, Sitting Bull's brother, and his followers were stopped in route to meet other Lakota chiefs. He was stopped by the 7th Calvary. His tribe was escorted about 5 miles to make camp near Wounded Knee Creek. On December 29, 1890, the army went into the camp to disarm all the Indians. There were 500 troops that surrounded the Indian encampment with 4 Hotchkiss guns that were rapid fire guns.

When the soldiers tried to disarm Black Coyote, who was deaf, Black Coyote refused to give his gun up. The Indians tried to tell the soldiers that Black Coyote was deaf and didn't understand why the men were wanting his gun. He said that he had paid much money for this gun and wanted to keep it. Two of the soldiers grabbed Black Coyote from behind. Coyote's gun discharged into the air not harming anyone. One of the officers gave the command to open fire on the Indians.

Most of the Indians had been disarmed. They tried to fight back but were massacred by the Army. Over 300 Indian men, women and children were killed with 51 wounded. The Army had only 25 dead, with 39 wounded. Most of the military soldiers died from friendly fire.

I arrived there shortly after. I had been visiting my wife's relatives at the Pine Ridge Reservation when I heard about the 7th Calvary being on the march. I tried to stop it, but I was too late. What I saw was unimageable. Indian men, women and children were killed and shot many times. Soldiers cut off body parts. The soldiers had gone mad with blood lust. I won't describe the horror I saw.

My wife was near my children. I had a young son and daughter. Their names were White Dove, my wife, Brown Bear, my son and Yellow Bird, my daughter. My son and daughter were already dead from many bullets from the rapid-fire guns. My wife was wounded. I thought she could still be saved. She was out of her mind with grief.

My wife said, "I cannot let my children cross the Rainbow bridge alone. They will need me. I must go to them." I told her that they would be all right. Sitting Bull is there. He will take care of them. My wife took out her skinning knife and put it close to her heart.

I will always remember what she said to me. It seems just like yesterday. Her lying on the grassy ground with the knife at her heart. "I must go to my babies. I have to be near them. They are so young. They will not understand. Please John, my husband, help me be with them. I don't have the strength to do it myself. The Great Spirit will understand what you must do. I will die anyway. Please, John, I must go before they cross the Rainbow bridge. Do it for them! That's when I took her hand and helped her die. I looked at the sky. She was walking with our two children holding their hands. Sitting Bull held out his hand and helped them cross the bridge. She turned and smiled back at me. I took my children and wife here to be buried. The Great Elder and Council were kind to allow me that.

I promised to protect this land with my dying breath. All warriors should protect this land. It is one of the last of its kind. Tonight, I had the honor of seeing my family one last time. Sitting Bull reminded me of that promise I made. I know that the Great Council had the dance in my honor and to honor my friends: **The Keepers of the Yawi**. I will honor my promise or die trying."

John with tears in his eyes handed the Talking Stick back to the Great Elder. To everybody's surprise, the Great Elder handed the Talking Stick to Antonio. Antonio stood up, "I was there, too. I was working as a scout for the 7th Calvary. I heard the sound of gunfire. I rode to a ridge overlooking Wounded Knee. John didn't know I was working for the Army. I watched it all, but I could do nothing. I did not want to tell John. Some things are better left unsaid.

For many years, I have tried to forget what I saw that day. It changed my life. I tried not to have any feelings after seeing man's inhumanity. It is now the time when I must come to terms with it.

I will do whatever I need to ensure the survival of this land. I couldn't do anything then, but I can now. John is my blood brother. I will follow him anywhere. This meeting has reminded me of what happens when evil dominants. This land and what it means is too important. We must succeed."

Not a sound could be heard. Nobody expected what had happened. The Great Elder took back the Talking Stick. Nobody needed to say more. All that needed to be said had been said.

A woman's voice could be heard. It was gentle like a new songbird. "John, we love you. You must go on and learn to love. I was lucky to have you as my husband and your children. You need someone to love you again. You need to love your child that is here. You know who he is. The Red Woman has raised him, and you have helped her. Go with my heart and love. We will always love you." It was almost too heartbreaking when both of his children could be heard saying, "Daddy, we love you." The room became silent again. The Council stood up and left. They were satisfied with the answers they got tonight.

The Council room was quiet. The group was stunned with the revelations that they saw and heard. There wasn't a person among them that didn't have a tear in their eye. Antonio got up and motioned for the rest of the group to leave. John and Antonio had some talking to do.

The rest of the group filed out of the room. Red Woman met them and took them to another part of the great cave. There were beds on the floor for everyone to sleep on. Lo Ming told everyone that they would have a meeting while John and Antonio were gone.

John was finally able to speak. "Why didn't you tell me that you were there?" Antonia replied, "I thought you already knew. I thought that was why you chose me. I always wondered why you didn't blame me. I left the 7th Calvary that day. I saw you from a distance. I saw the Rainbow Bridge in the sky. You lost everything there."

"When we exchanged blood, we became blood brothers. We have no choice. We must protect each other. Antonio, I know many things about you. I have knowledge of many things. I never knew you were there. I know now that I must tell you something that could make you hate me," said John in a whisper.

"You have earned the right to know this. I thought I would never tell you. I thought you would never deserve to know. You are my blood brother. I am bound to tell you." John said looking into Antonio's eyes. "What is that, John?" asked Antonio. "You may have guessed it or felt it. I saw how you and Angela have looked at him," replied John. "You mean One Feather. I felt that we had a connection," whispered Antonio. "You do. He is your son. Angela took him to a home for boys when he was born. She didn't know that I took him here to be with his Great Grandfather, The Great Elder. Angela is The Great Elder's Granddaughter. She doesn't know about this. Remember, she didn't know where you had gone and couldn't find you." Instead of being mad, Antonio was too shocked to say anything.

John was waiting to see Antonio's reaction to what he had been told. "I guess at that time I wouldn't have been much of a father. I was too jaded with life. Angela never told me about having a son. I can't blame her. Did you raise him like a son? Antonio asked. "No, I didn't. I raised him like I was always his uncle. He was your son. That was why I chose you. You had to know. You had to help save him with me. It is your duty as a father and my duty also." Antonio had tears in his eyes. "I understand more than you will ever know. I read it in *The Book of Spring.* I just didn't believe it. It was our destiny. It will take time for me to get over what you have done. I can't change anything. We will see how this goes. Nobody will ever hurt my son and his mother. That is all I can tell you. I meant what I said. I will follow you or die trying. That was written in the books. My son must keep his uncle." Antonio left John to himself.

The others had their meeting. They were in shock. Lo Ming said, "I was not surprised about anything. This journey has proven to be unpredictable. John and Antonio must be hundreds of years old. I knew that both of them had secrets. That doesn't bother me. We have to stay together. We have learned a lot. We have much to learn. I know that now I understand John's motivation. I still do not understand why we were chosen. I feel it is our destiny to follow him."

Rose stated that she would do as John had done if it had been her. "I have another reason to be here. John is giving me a chance to find my first love. A man named Zan. Nick knows about him. He has stated that he will help me. He is somewhere in this land. You may think it is selfish of me to say that I will follow John, but I would follow anyone that loves his family as much as he did." Rose choked on her tears. Nick nodded, "I found my first love because of John. I owe him that much." Mary said, "I have seen a different John tonight. I will stay with him, but I don't know quite why." Moses started to say something. Lo Ming stopped him. "Moses, you must forgive John. He is here to save his friend, your father. Your mother told me that. He saved your mother. He promised your father he would come back and save him. Put down your hate. You are here to help get your father back. I love you, Moses. I love your mother. I know I will love your father. I only hope you still love me." Moses didn't say anything. He just stood up and took Lo Ming into his arms and kissed her. "I have no choice because I love you more than life," cried Moses with tears running down his face.

That was all that needed said. Everyone was in agreement. June didn't say anything. She didn't have to. Everyone knew she loved One Feather. That meant this land was her land. They only needed John and Antonio to return. After all, Nick said what everyone was thinking, "We are **The Keepers of the Yawi.**"

Chapter IV
What comes next?

A young woman came into the room where everyone was waiting for John and Antonio to return. She motioned for Lo Ming and Moses to follow her. They didn't question her. They just followed her. She took them to another room down the hallway. A blanket covered the entrance to that room. The young woman pulled the blanket to the side for them to enter. The room was lit with torches in each corner. There were wool and linen blankets on the floor. The Red Woman was standing by the side of the makeshift bed.

"This room is for you and Moses. Lo Ming, you made a very difficult, unselfish act to leave Moses behind. To go against the wishes of one you love is hard. We know that you thought it was best to have him stay, but you chose for Moses to stay.

This can make any relationship almost impossible to survive. To show our gratitude, we have given you this room for your use. Both of you fulfilled a prophesy that was written long ago. It foretold of a warrior woman from the east and a brave dark man like a strong buffalo from the distant South willing to sacrifice everything for our land. We have furnished food, drink and some other things that should make this night special for you," smiled the red woman as she left the room.

Lo Ming put her arms around Moses. He was about to kiss her when she threw him over her shoulder like a wrestler into the bed. She jumped on top of him and held him down. "What did you do that for?" Moses asked. "Your mother gave me two orders to make you love me, again. One was to beat you up, and the other was to make love to you until you were too tired to complain. It's now time for the lovemaking part, if you are up to it, old man," whispered Lo Ming. Moses smiled back at Lo Ming. "I will show you, I'm no old man."

June hoped to see One Feather. After about an hour, One Feather walked into the room. He motioned for June to follow him. "Don't wait on me," said June as she left with him. Nick decided to get some sleep. He took off most of his clothes except for his underwear. Mary asked him if it was alright to examine his burns. She was pleased that the burns were healing. Rose noticed that the burns on his leg resembled a male deer with large antlers. She wondered if that burn would stay that way. Mary noticed the same thing. "Nick, it looks like the burn on your leg will give you a permanent tattoo. I hope that you won't mind a big stag deer. You will have to ask June what that means," said Mary. "At least, it's not some naked girl," he replied.

It had been two days since Angela had made it back to the edge of the forest. Across the field was the entrance to the tunnel that could take her back to Eagle Train Station. She had decided to wait here at the edge of the forest. It was too dangerous to try to make it to the tunnel. The field still had hidden crevices and holes that had lava in them.

She had started a campfire and cooked some vegetables that she had found on the trail back. She had a small canteen quart aluminum cup to cook in. She put some water with the vegetables and made a soup. She had set up her camp so she could sit down and lean against a log. She looked at the stars in the night's sky. She ate her soup.

She missed Antonio. He was the love of her life. She had some regrets in her life. The biggest was giving up their son for adoption. She had tried to find Antonio, but he was gone after she was arrested in Italy. Antonio never knew that they had a son. It was a long story. When she realized the mistake she had made, she went to get her son back. The nuns told her that a man had already claimed him. He had a letter from the Pope that said to give the child to him. They didn't know who he was or where he was from. She tried to find him, but there were no leads. It was as if they had vanished.

She knew their son was probably a full-grown man now. Her thoughts turned to One Feather. There was something about him that drew her to him. There was something familiar about him. She kept searching her mind about that fact. In her knap shack, she reached in. She pulled out an old picture she had taken of Antonio those many years ago. The campfire gave her some light. Something jumped out at her. It was the sparking eyes of Antonio. She had seen those eyes before. She closed her eyes to think where. One picture came to her mind's eye. It was the young brave, One Feather. Antonio and One Feather had the same eyes. How could that be?

The earth started to shake. Angela jumped up. The field in front of her waved like an ocean. The cracks in the land filled up. The boulders moved back into their place on the mountain.

Everything was moving in reverse. The land was healing itself. The Red Woman had told her to be careful. Mysterious things could be happening in the next few days. This must be the result of the ceremony they were having for John's group. Something big must have happened. She watched the trees spring up and return to normal. In a few moments, it was if the earthquake had never happened. The land was new again. She turned around and looked at Eagle Mountain. The mountain had many lights on its top. She could hear faint sounds of drums. Yes, it had to be the ceremony.

It had become peaceful again. She sat down. She thought of Shanna. She owed Shanna a lot. Antonio told her how Shanna had saved his life by risking hers. She smiled. For some reason, Shanna and she had become close. Maybe it was that they were so much alike. Both of them were very independent. They liked adventure. They were free spirits. Their word was their bond. When they talked at night around the campfire, they realized that they were in love with men that they had thought they had lost. They made a pact. It would be their responsibility to make sure, if possible, to keep each other's love safe when the other was not around. Shanna had kept her promise. Angela would keep hers.

Antonio had told her one more thing about Shanna. He told Angela that the way Shanna had told him that she promised Angela she would keep him safe could only mean one thing. Angela loved him. Shanna would have never put her life in danger for him for anything less. Antonio told Angela that it made him realize that he loved Angela. Angela did owe Shanna more than Shanna would ever know.

Angela looked across the field in front of her. The field was healed. Everything was in its rightful place. She had a feeling that she must go back to Houston right away. She must see Shanna. The feeling she had was not good. Something could happen to Shanna. Shanna had created some very powerful enemies saving Antonio and David. Now, it was her turn to return the favor.

I looked at the bright star lit sky. The moon was bright red. I thought about the people that I had brought to this land over the years. I had chosen individuals that were famous in various academic fields, even the occult. None of these groups survived the challenges they faced.

It wasn't until I realized the individuals, I chose had to have something more. This land is a spiritual and mystical land. I never had realized that was the key. One day at the Eagle Train Station I was talking to the old man. The group that I took did not work out. Several had died in the trip to **The Land of the Eagle Feathers**. I can still remember what the old man said, "Knowledge is one thing. Knowledge is good, but there is something more powerful than knowledge. It is the spirit in the person that is more powerful. History has shown that if someone has a connection to what they are fighting for, they can overcome the odds against them. They will fight harder. I have seen it happen many times. A spiritual connection is often the difference in winning. John, answer this question, why do you fight so hard for this land? The old man and his dog left me to think about it. I knew the answer to that question. It was for my family and friends. The old man was right.

I chose a different type of group many years ago. Each individual had a spiritual connection with this land. They were special. Each had a reason to come with me. We were not looking for the Sacred Books at that time. We were only trying to save this land. This group fought well. We had a bond. Several died in saving it from those that would have exploited it.

We were powerful in battle. However, we were only just powerful enough to stop them. I told them to go home and learn more and to teach their powers to another person. They would have to choose that person based on their abilities. Some chose their own blood relatives. Some chose other individuals. The group of people that I have with me now have that spiritual connection. They do not know it. They will find out about it soon. Their teachers have taught them well. The only problem is that this group have many demons of their own. Which wolf they will choose will determine whether we live or die?

The morning sun was rising in the east. Its color was red with some dark clouds hiding its glow. Rose looked at the sunrise. She didn't like its meaning. A storm was brewing. She was wondering if the red sunrise meant more than just a storm. It could mean that things could be getting more stressful for the group. After last night's council, things were starting to change. People were looking at John differently. He had hidden his reasons for saving this land. Everyone knew that last night only scratched the surface of who John was. Antonio was much more than anyone could have guessed. We knew the others would be thinking the same.

Everyone had gotten up for breakfast. A full meal had been placed outside around a campfire. There were several fruits to pick from with eggs and cornbread and honey. They were all together for the first time. Moses, Lo Ming, June and One Feather had joined them. Antonio had just arrived. The last one to join them was John. Rose and Nick were making small talk.

Nick asked Moses, "How did you and One Feather survive these weeks? When did you meet up with Angela?" Moses had been very tight lipped about what had happened to them. Everyone had waited for Moses to tell them. Moses took a deep breath and told them the story.

"Lo Ming said that you know most of it from Rose's crystal ball. When I was pushed out of the tunnel, the whole ground started shaking. Rocks came down the mountainside. I knew that I couldn't get back to the tunnel safely. I saw One Feather in the distance running toward the woods. Knowing he knew this land better than I; I ran after him. We had made it close to the wood line when a powerful wave of the earthquake hit. A large Oak tree fell on top of us. We had tried to get away, but it took us by surprise. I was pinned by one large branch that fell on my right leg. One Feather was hit by another branch that broke his arm. One Feather couldn't lift the branch off me. I was starting to bleed from a wound caused by a sharp point of the branch. I couldn't move. One Feather stopped the bleeding by putting pressure on my wound. We both knew we were in a terrible situation. I was pinned to the ground bleeding, and One Feather couldn't help much with a bad arm.

After about an hour, we had about given up hope. Out of the dark forest came a figure of a woman. We knew who she was once she spoke to us. "I see you have gotten yourselves into some trouble. I guess I must try to save you two. You know I won't let you ever live this down." Angela had a wicked smile on her face. She seemed to enjoy us being helpless. She didn't look much better than us. She was dirty with dust and mud, covering most of her body.

She had a small camp shovel in her backpack. She was able to dig under the branch and get my leg out. She knew what she was doing. She was fast and efficient. She cleaned up my wounds. She took out a needle and some fishing line. It wasn't the most pleasant of experiences. She got the bleeding stopped. I didn't know she could sew so well.

She made a sling for One Feather's arm. She told One Feather it was only a fracture and not to move it much or it would get worse. She had One Feather gather some firewood. We made camp there for several days. She did most of the work. She made one large tent out of ours. She cleaned our clothes and helped bathe and wash us. She cooked what was left of our food. I never had seen that side of Angela before. She was like a mother hen taking care of her flock. One thing she was worried about was Antonio. I told her that I thought he had gotten out alright. That seemed to satisfy her.

She didn't talk too much about anything about her. I never asked her how she got here. She didn't tell us anything. One day she noticed something about my leg. She told us that we needed to move. We had to find Red Woman. She said that I was getting Red Fever. If I didn't get proper medicine, it could kill me. One Feather had totally recovered from his injuries. You know the rest. One Feather and I owe Angela a lot. She saved us. No matter what Angela does or who she is, we must protect her. It is our duty."

One Feather looked at me. "John, you know the legend about a young girl that was banished from **The Land of the Eagle Feathers** by the Great Elder. Could Angela be that girl?" I told him that I had heard of such a legend. I told them that only Angela could tell us that. I could tell that they knew I had not told them everything. They were smart enough to put the pieces together. I told them that tonight there would be a meeting with the Red Woman on the ridgetop. Rose told everyone that a storm would hit in about an hour. We would need to stay inside most of the day.

It started thundering about an hour later. Rain came down in sheets. Lightning flashed between the clouds. The thunder roared down the valleys. Nick watched the storm. He liked to hear the rain. It reminded him of a time that Shanna and he had to run into a shelter by the seashore. They were wet and young. He had found some driftwood in the shelter and made a fire. They had watched the storm and its dark clouds over the ocean. They held each other as the rain hit the tin roof of the shelter. Nick nodded to himself. "Yes, I do like the sound of the rain. I do miss her very much." Rose was sitting beside him. "You miss Zan as much as I miss Shanna. Don't you?" said Nick. Rose could only nod. "Don't worry. We will find him. I promise you that. I keep my promises like Shanna kept hers to Angela."

They left for the ridgetop when the full moon was rising in the dark night's sky. There was a campfire burning with several logs as benches on the ridgetop. They sat down on the logs and waited. The moon was the blood moon. It was large and a light red. This was a sacred time in **The Land of the Eagle Feathers**. It was when the moon reached overhead that she came.

The Red Woman's buckskin dress was white with crystal beads of all colors. The moonlight shimmered on the crystals. Her face had a red glow. In her dark hair were white crystals beads on strands of dark string. She looked like a goddess from an age long ago.

"I come to you to answer some of your questions. You have wondered why you are here. I know why. John did not tell you how he picked you. I assisted him. Every one of you have a connection to this place. Some of you have ancestors here. Some of you have family that fought for us. Moses, you have an Indian name. We have watched you. We call you, "He-who talks-to-Animals. Your great-great-grandfather was at Wounded Knee. He was in the Calvary. He had been assigned from the group of soldiers called the Buffalo Soldiers. That is what we called them. They had the hair of our sacred Buffalo. They were fierce warriors. They treated us as equals. When your great-great-grandfather saw what was happening, he tried to get the soldiers to stop firing. They didn't pay him any attention. The word was that he had gone missing in the fighting. We know different. He left the scene and left America. He went as far away as possible. He ended up in

Australia. He went to the Outback. He became one with the natives. There is one more thing. Your father and mother fought with John and saved this land several years ago. We honor them as great warriors. You can bring your father back if you obtain *The Book of Winter*. His spirit is with us.

Rose, your great grandfather was a physician. He arrived at Wounded Knee after the fighting. He saw the aftermath of the fighting. He worked for a while at the Pine Ridge Reservation. He couldn't forget. They say that he went to the swamps of the lower Mississippi. Nobody had contact with him after that. Your father and mother fought with John. They too helped to save this land. It is said that you have greater powers than your parents. You have other reasons to be here. You have other fights to fight.

June, your tribe was once here and lived in these lands. They have a mixed association with us. They fought for many years to keep this land. They left when they lost too many warriors. They feared that their tribe would be lost. We can only hope that they will return to us. Your father and grandfather have taught you well. You are a gifted Shaman. You are the only one that can defeat Red Bear and lift the curse on your tribe. We know that you have other reasons to find the books as well.

Nick, you are a great warrior. Your ancestors once lived here before moving West. We had hope that they would return to us. Your grandfather has taught you well. They, too, have been here long ago. Your grandfather was a great warrior. Destiny has called you here. You need to heal those wounds of war. You must finish what you have started. You will find out what I mean when your journey here is over.

Mary, you have many great demons within you. Can you be trusted to finish this journey? We do not know. Your memory has been corrupted. You must find the answers to your memories to fulfill your destiny. Your dreams have told you who is your son. I am your mother. David is your father. I will not tell you more. You will have to find the last book to find your answer to who your son's father is. Your mixed blood could be a blessing or a curse.

To everyone here, I cannot tell you about Angela. She has many demons to fight within herself. I only hope that she finds her way back. She, too, has a son here. She does not know it. She is a scorpion. You must watch her carefully. Much like you must watch everyone in your group.

Lo Ming, you are a great warrior. One of the greatest we have ever seen. Why you are here only John knows. I cannot tell you. Perhaps, it is because of fate. You will find out your destiny when you find the last book. You have sacrificed many things in your life. Your uncle fought for us many years ago. That is not why you are here. Only destiny and time will tell you.

The Book of Fall will be very difficult to find. The passages that you have been given are more symbolism than a map. You will have to use your intelligence more than your physical powers to find it.

You need to know one more thing. From now on, things will get more dangerous. You have many enemies that will stop at nothing to destroy you. To give you more powers, we have decided to make this journey of yours a Vision Quest. By doing that, you are entitled to have a Medicine Bag. The Great Elder will tell you how to do a Medicine Bag. I wish you well. May the spirits be with you. I hope to see you in next season. Antonio, give me *The Book of Summer.*" Antonio pulled it from under his shirt. He laid it on a stone in front of the Red Woman. The Red Woman took the book and faded into the night. Antonio looked at Moses. "I almost forgot. Here is your passage, Moses. You know what to do with it."

He walked out of the darkness into the firelight. The Great Elder held up his hand. In it his hand was an eagle feather. He pointed the eagle feather at the fire, and it went out. "We need no fire light tonight only the rays of the moon and bright sparkling of the stars and planets. I have come to give you the knowledge you must have to complete the Vision Quest for the last two books.

Time is growing short for us all. The Dark Ones and others will soon be coming into **The Land of the Eagle Feathers.** We cannot hold them back much longer. You must find *The Book of Fall*. Then return and find *The Book of Winter* before the rise of the New Year's moon," he said in a voice that had a hint of urgency in it.

The Great Elder was accompanied by One Feather and the young boy. The Great Elder spoke again in a voice that demanded everyone's attention. The Council recognizes that each of you have powers of your own. However, they also recognize that to survive it will take all of your collected strengths and powers. We will help give you more power for you to succeed. I will remind you that if you don't work together, if any of you fail to assist the others of your group, you will fail. Failure is not an option for any of us. Failure will result in the loss of this land and the ending of your life's journey.

If you survive and find *The Book of Fall*, you must have one of these. He pointed to the ground in front of each of them. There appeared a leather bag with a shoulder strap. "Before you are your medicine bags," he pointed out. This is important. It is written in the stars that the last books will be a Vision Quest. You cannot begin a Vision Quest without a medicine bag. Your medicine bag will give you more power to protect you on that journey. It must be filled with objects that represent you. There are objects you must have and objects that represent your spirit.

   In each bag, there are two pouches. In one pouch put some cornmeal. In the other pouch, place a piece of flint which will represent fire or the light of your spirit. The following items are basic items you must include:

1. One or more of stones, minerals or crystals that you choose.
2. One or more items relating to animals such as: a feather, claw, bone or fur.
3. One or more items relating to plants or trees such as leaves, bark, roots or stems.
4. Finally, one object that represents where you came from.

   Do not fill you medicine bag completely. You will need to leave room for the special objects that you will find on the Vision Quest for *The Book of Winter*. **Remember that each type of item or object you take is up to you. They need to represent your spirit. You must choose wisely because this is where your powers will come from to assist you to complete the Quest for *The Book of Winter*.**

   Now for the knowledge about what a Quest is; since the beginning of time in **The Land of the Eagle Feathers** we have held Quests. Some of these quests were for young people's rite of passage to become adults. Some quests were conducted to give a person great medicine or to make them wise to become great leaders. Some quests were to grant special insights into the future. This quest will have two goals: one is for the power to save this land from the evil of men, and the other is for the boy over there. Only the Great Spirits know where each of your paths will lead. The final part of the Vision Quest will begin here, the first night of the Winter Season. After 9 cycles of days, it must end here with *The Book of Winter*.

The Great Elder pointed to the young boy at his side. "This boy will be going with you on this Vision Quest. It is his Vision Quest to become a man." It was the young boy that we had seen before. There was something different about the boy. The boy's eyes were special. They were not brown but of different colors depending how you looked at them. His right eye had a yellow glowing tint that emulated behind it. Everyone noticed it and recognized he was not just a young boy. You could see that he was about the age he would become a young man. He was a boy at the age of transition. Mary could feel something about the boy. She knew in her heart that he was her son. I could feel it too.

As the Elder, One Feather and young boy were about to walk away into the darkness of the night forest, the Elder spoke once more. "In this **Land of the Eagle Feathers**, the Spirits of this land are great and wise. What you chose for your medicine bag and your deeds and visions during the quest will determine your life's path. We will meet again on the first night of the Winter Season to begin the final part of the Vision Quest. I hope that you find *The Book of Fall*. If you don't, it will not matter. Leave the boy here if you do. He would have passed the first test to be a man."

Everyone sat in silence. You could almost hear their thoughts in the mountain wind. We were all one now together like a band or tribe. We would face the test of the Vision Quest together. Everything was going to depend on being successful in our Quest. This land depended on us to succeed. We would be here the first night of the Winter Season. No matter who or what would try to stop us.

Everyone in the group gazed at the bright stars and moon. It was as if you could hear their thoughts. Moses' heart ached to see his father again. He was still mad at his mother for not telling him the whole story of what happened to his father.

They had never told him about his ancestors. He knew a little about his mother's. She was a descendant of Genghis Khan. Many people are, but she believes that she is a direct descendant.

His father and grandfather didn't talk much about the past. His grandfather was a great medicine man in the aborigine tribes of Australia. His grandmother died before he was born. He had mixed feelings about John. He would let that go for now and see what happens. He was grateful for one thing. He would never have met Lo Ming if it hadn't been for John. He wondered how Lo Ming fit into this picture. His grandfather taught him to be patient. His grandfather often talked about your destiny is written in the stars of the night's sky.

Rose often wondered why his father and mother lived in the swamps of Louisiana. There were many places that were much more suitable to live. Her father is a Wizard. He was known to be one of the greatest. He had a funny nickname. People called him Big Crawdaddy. Her mother was a Voodoo Priestess. She was also one of the greatest skilled Priestess that every lived. Rose was lucky to have studied both sides of her parents' skills. That gave her an advantage over many magicians or wizards. She could only hope that John would help her find Zan, her lover. If he couldn't, surely her parents could.

Nick liked adventure. He loved Shanna. He was worried about her. He hoped that she was recovering from her wounds. To say that his life was complicated would be an understatement. His grandfather had told him that he was descended from great warriors. His grandfather told him that it was his mind that would make him victorious in battle. He knew that John picked him for two reasons. One was for his skills, and the other was for Shanna. He didn't know why, but he could wait to find out his destiny.

June had many reasons for being here. She knew about her tribe's weakness. They left the last battle before it ended. Her grandfather told her that she was the only one that could rectify this stain on her tribe. She was in love with One Feather. She knew One Feather was in love with her. Destiny had drawn them together. She had guessed who One Feather's parents were. Eyes always tell the truth. One Feather had Antonio's eyes. Angela went to great pains to save One Feather. She also knew that Angela didn't know she was One Feather's mother. Angela would figure it out sooner or later. Mothers always do. She only hoped that it wouldn't be too much of a shock for One Feather. She would help him if he needed help. To have Angela and Antonio as in-laws would not be easy.

Mary was still at a loss for all that had happened. A few weeks ago, everything seemed so easy. David and she had it all planned out. They would steal the last book and take over. They would be so powerful that nobody could stop them. She wanted to talk to David about her mother, the Red Woman. David refused to talk to her about it. As much as she wanted to know, she knew that she would have to find out for herself about her parents' past. Her instincts told her that the young boy was her son. The boy's father was a different story. She had no idea. Her mother told her that the answer was written in the last book, *The Book of Winter*. She didn't know whether to follow her father or her mother. She would have to decide for herself. One thing was clear. The only path that she would ever choose would be to protect her son. How better to protect him than be the most powerful person in the world. She knew that her father and she would have to defeat Raven and Benita to survive. That would be the first thing to do.

Lo Ming was one that wasn't given a reason to be here. Her uncle had fought with John. She knew that wasn't the reason for her being here. There had to be something else. She was in love with Moses. She knew he loved her. Maybe when we got back, she could get answers from Van Sing, her uncle. She doubted it. The last book had the answer. She would have to live long enough to find the answer. She wasn't as patient as Moses. She would just have to wait.

Antonio had many questions that needed answered. He was somewhat confused. He was not angry at Angela. It was as much his fault as hers. He would play the hand he was dealt. How was he going to tell Angela? Maybe she would guess it before he had to tell her. As he looked at the stars, he wondered which wolf would he choose? He only hoped the right one.

The Red Woman was pleased to see how everyone was woven into the same destiny. Everyone owed another one their life or something else. John and she had picked the right ones. It was mostly John's doing. She didn't agree with John, but she knew he was right. John would be looking to find her. He would be very angry with her for holding so much from him. Perhaps, it would be better if she disappeared for a while.

Arguing with him would settle nothing. John would have to deal with this situation by himself. After all, it was his plan that started this whole thing in motion. Now it was up to the great spirits to help him find his way. There was one place she had to go. It would be very dangerous for her to go there. She smiled; David would be shocked to see her. She had a score to settle with him. John would never guess that she would ever go to Houston.

I looked for the Red Woman. I could not find her. Finally, I decided to go to the Great Elder for answers. "Why are you here, John? the Great Elder asked. Before I could answer, the Great Elder stated, "I already know the answer. You want to talk to the Red Woman. She is not here. She left two hours ago. She did not say. I think it has something to do with her past life. We all have unfinished business. Don't we, John?" I looked at the Great Elder. "You are looking for answers to questions that I cannot answer for you," the Great Elder replied. "Why didn't she tell me about the boy? I asked. "She had her reasons. At that time, you were not in the best frame of mind. Your heart was full of hate and despair. Also, we did not know if you were going to survive the battle with the **Dark Ones**. Maybe, our decision not to tell you could be questioned. We used your anger. We knew that you would want to strike out at David. Revenge is a powerful weapon. We felt that when you got that out of your spirit, we might trust you with your son. The problem was that you have never gotten it out of your system. Have you, John?"

I didn't need to answer his question. The Great Elder was right. I had used every military strategy that I had learned over the years. I borrowed from my time with the Roman Legions to the Great War in Europe. It was Indian Plains Wars that taught me the most. "Yes, I can see your point. At least, I got to spend time with him. I always treated him like my son," I answered his question. "We knew you were once a good father. You always were. Little Wolf looked at you as if you were his father. You should remember. We did not know how long your transition from being dead to life would last. You have only a short time left. If you do not find *The Book of Winter* and its secrets by the New Year's moon, you will fade and die like a ghost into the night," the Great Elder reminded me.

"It would do you no good to argue with the Red Woman. Be glad that your son, Little Wolf, is going with you. His destiny is in your hands. You are blessed to get to be part of his Vision Quest to become a man. Remember, do not tell his mother, Mary, anything. She must discover for herself.

Mary is not the shy young woman you knew long ago. You know that deep down in your soul. Everyone of your group is like the Indian Fable about the Raven and the Wolf. Have June tell everyone that fable one night on the trail. They will need to recognize the truth in it. You must leave at first light to find *The Book of Fall.* The stars and planets have aligned for you to find it. Don't tell Little Wolf about you. Don't worry, he already sees you in his mind as his father. You have taught him well over the years here. Take One Feather with you. We had made him one of your group. Last night, we had a ceremony to make him one of **The Keepers of the Yawi**. He has the mark of the Eagle on the back of his hand."

Chapter V
The Vision Quest Starts:
Where is *The Book of Fall?*

As the first light of dawn came from behind the Great Mountain, we were on our way down the mountain. I told everyone that One Feather was now part of our group. He showed everyone the back of his hand. "This is Little Wolf. He is going with us. It is his Vision Quest to become a man." I asked Antonio who had the first passage for our way to find the book. He said that Nick had the first passage this time. "When we get down this mountain, we start on the journey. Remember, there will be many trials this time. The spirits will not help us. In fact, they will be testing us. Be on your guard at all times," I told them. It was late morning when we reached the base of Eagle Mountain. I asked Antonio again, "Who's passage is the first to follow?" Antonio replied, "Nick."

Nick recited his Passage to the group.

For the Love of Your Brother

What would you do
For one other than you
What would you do for another
For the love of your brother

If one piece of bread were left
Would you eat it yourself
If the fight had already begun
Would you leave him and run

If he were drowning in the river
Would you stand there and shiver
If the snake was by his side
Would you run away and hide

If he was attacked by a bear
Would you stand there and stare
If it could cost you your life
Would you be willing to take a knife

No matter who you are
The answers are on the South Star
It tells you what you should do
The rest is up to you.

Nick looked at us. He said, "What I got out of this passage was that we need to go to a river called The Drowning River. We should follow the South Star. When we get there, we need to find a large rock formation that looks like a large Bear." Before One Feather could say anything, Little Wolf blurted out, "I know that place. The Great Elder took me there once. I can lead us there. I once played on that rock formation." One Feather didn't say anything. He knew that this Quest was Little Wolf's Vision Quest. He knew where this was. He would make sure that Little Wolf wouldn't get them lost.

Little Wolf said that it would take us two days of hard walking to get there. He knew a good place to camp about half a day's walk from here. I told him to lead the way, but to be careful. I signaled Nick to walk closely behind Little Wolf. Nick has a sense of danger if something wasn't right. I thought the meaning to this passage was too easy. Something about it was not right.

The going was a little rough. The trail we followed was rocky. The terrain was hilly to mountainous. We would walk uphill for a thousand feet and then back down. This happened several times. When we came to a steep cliff on one side of the trail, I told everyone to tie ourselves together. The trail was very slick and wet. One wrong move could cause you to slip over the edge and fall a thousand feet below. One Feather whispered to Little Wolf to go very slow.

Being young, Little Wolf did not listen to him. He went too fast. Nick suddenly pulled hard on the lead rope that was attached to Little Wolf. A large boulder came crashing down the side of the trail just in front of Little Wolf. This caused Little Wolf to slip over the side of the cliff. Nick immediately sat down and braced himself. He put his feet on two large embedded rocks on the trail. Everyone in our group did the same thing. This stopped anyone else from sliding off the trail.

One Feather yelled for Little Wolf. "I am all right. The rope is holding me. I can't get a foothold to pull me up." We were all relieved to hear his voice. Nick shouted for Little Wolf not to move. He was afraid that the sharp rocks could cut the rope. "Someone will have to climb down and get Little Wolf. I can hold him. Who wants to volunteer to get him?" Antonio stated that he would do it. He had a lot of experience climbing mountains in the Swiss Alps. Being at the end of the safety line behind the rest of us, it made a lot of sense for him to go anyway.

Antonio took off his pack. He had a small rope that he kept in his pack. He moved very slowly to the edge of the cliff where

Little Wolf had gone over. It was very slick and muddy there. Antonio looked over the edge. We heard him whistle. "He is down about 15 feet. His rope has a cut in it. This is going to be very tricky. I will have to free climb down to get him. Don't jerk on his safety rope. It will break the rope."

Antonio, very slowly, started over the side. He moved as if in slow motion. His skills as a climber was all that stood between Little Wolf coming back alive or falling to his death. After a short time, Antonio could be heard telling Little Wolf to grab hold of the short rope he was throwing him. A few seconds later, Nick shouted to everyone to hold tight. A large boulder had started to fall just in front of him. We held the rope as tight as possible. As the boulder went over the side, our rope became slack. We knew what that meant. The safety rope on Little Wolf had broken. We heard Little Wolf yell. Then, there was silence. Nobody said a word. We were all thinking, "Did we lose both Antonio and Little Wolf?"

After a few long moments, a hand rose out of the edge of the cliff trail. Antonio pulled himself up with a young passenger on his back. It was Little Wolf. Nick gave them a hand and assisted them up. Smiles came to our faces. Nick motioned for all of us to move back down the trail. Soon we were off the cliff. What Nick said next shocked us, "Someone had booby-trapped the trail. Those rocks had been set to fall. I saw a trip rope attached to the last boulder that came down."

"I thought that this was too easy. The spirits are testing us or someone else knows where we are going. Is there another way to get there?" I asked. One Feather nodded, yes. I told him to take the lead that we would follow him. He stated that it would take several more hours to get to a place to camp for the night. I gave him the sign to lead the way. I could see that Mary was shaken by what had just happened. This told me that she knew more about Little Wolf than I thought. The only thing that was said was by Nick, "I should have paid more attention to the line. It could have cost you your life."

I put Nick and Moses in the back of the line. If we would have any more trouble, it would come from behind us. Little Wolf was upset at having slipped off the trail. I told him that it wasn't his fault. I told him he was brave in not losing his control and keeping calm. I did scold him for not paying attention to what One Feather had told him. "I know. I will listen more carefully," he replied.

We backtracked a mile or more. One Feather found a faint trail to our left. It looked like it hadn't been traveled on for several years. It was partly overgrown with small brush and trees that were beginning to take over the trail. June stated, "I liked this trail. If there is anyone ahead of us, they would leave signs on the trail." This trail was very difficult to hike. The brush was thick in places. We had to cut an opening on the trail in several places. We took turns in doing so, to keep everyone fresh and not get anyone too tired.

This untouched wilderness was a beautiful place. The mountain streams were full of trout. This part of the forest looked like it was thousands of years old. The trees were tall and with thick trunks. The late summer flowers were bright where the sun's rays would fall through holes in the forest canopy. I knew that we must be careful to not let this beauty distract us.

Nick and Moses signaled us to stop. Moses moved up to me, "We think someone is following us. Nick says about a mile behind us." One Feather signed that we had only about a mile to go to make camp in a meadow below us. I told everyone that we will camp there tonight. We must post guards because we could have an unexpected visitor.

I had Nick and Moses fall back from us. They were to try to find who was following. I told them not to take any chances in capturing whoever it was. It would be better to not let them know we know they are following. Besides if they want *The Book of Fall*, they would wait until we have it to do anything.

As we moved through the forest, June and Mary started to pick up several plants and dig some roots for our supper. There were wild mushrooms and berries everywhere. June found some wild sweet potatoes, onions and carrots in one section. This forest seemed magical in that if you thought of a vegetable it would appear by the trail. By the time we got to the meadow to camp for the night, they had collected enough vegetables to make vegetable soup.

We made camp and waited for Nick and Moses to appear. Lo Ming decided to cook. She had brought along several of her special spices for this very thing. She said that she had tired of food without the proper spices to make them taste better. When she added them to the soup, the smell was a wonderful aroma. Antonia and the rest of us found enough firewood to have a well-lit camp for the rest of the night.

It had just gotten dark when Moses and Nick found our camp. They didn't have much to tell us. Whoever was following us was very good at keeping their distance. They tried to get close to them, but they couldn't even get a single glimpse of them. They even swore that they thought the person must have mystical powers. They saw weeds and brush move beside the trail. They never saw what moved them. They did discover one track or footprint. It was a faint footprint of a moccasin. I told them to get something to eat. I would take the first watch. Then Antonio, Lo Ming, June, Little Wolf, Mary and finally Rose would take their turn to watch. I wanted Moses, Nick and One Feather to be fresh tomorrow.

I had everyone gather after Nick and Moses ate. I told June that the Great Elder wanted everyone to know the legend about *The Wolf and the Raven*. This legend was to be a lesson for all to hear. It was a beautiful night. The stars were bright against the dark night's sky. The campfire in the middle of our camp lit our tents up. Everyone got in a semi-circle with June in front of them. Just before June started, I left camp to keep watch. I chose a large boulder at the edge of camp to sit on top to watch June's storytelling and to watch the back trail for anyone that might come to visit us.

June was known in her tribe as a great storyteller. In Indian tribes, great storytellers were always in great demand. They would be the entertainment at night. Many mountain men would join in the activities. They said it was strange to have everyone laugh when nobody was talking. They used sign language when guests or another tribe's storyteller was visiting. The Indians enjoyed the mountain men that were friendly to them and traded with them. They liked that these men would exaggerate their stories. They were usually very funny stories. They also exaggerated their bravery and skills as fighters.

Jim Bridger, a famous mountain man, once told a story about being surrounded by a hundred fierce warriors. He was a great storyteller. The Native Indians asked him how the story ended. He laughed when he told them, naturally, I got killed. Even as great of a warrior I am, I couldn't beat one hundred warriors.

I watched silently as June started the legend of ***The Wolf and the Raven***. I could tell that she was really putting on a show for them. I could hear her from where I was. June had just started her story.

June enjoyed having an audience to tell a story to. She was in great demand as a lecturer on the college circuit on Native American Indian lore. She even changed into her Indian dress to tell the story. It went like this.

The Wolf and the Raven

Long ago, there lived a strong, powerful Wolf and a beautiful Raven. Each would come out at night. One night the Wolf saw the Raven and thought that was the most beautiful sight he had ever seen.

The Raven flew down to where the Wolf stood on a cliff. She said, "I am called Raven. He replied, "I am called Wolf. They frolicked each night together and fell deeply in love.

Finally, the day came when the Wolf asked the Raven to stay with him on the ground. The Raven told him that if he loved her, he would grow wings and come with her.

They stared at each other and realized that neither one could give up what they were for the other. They spent the rest of the night nestled together in silence. When the sun began to rise, they looked at each other with sadness. The Wolf ran into the forest, and the Raven flew into the skies.

That is why on clear nights when the moon is full, you hear the mournful call of the Wolf and the answering cry of the Raven.

As if planned by June, there was the howling of two wolves in the distance. Then a black Raven flew overhead and called her sad song. Nobody said a word. They just looked at each other. June made one more dramatic ending. "There is an Indian saying: Day and Night cannot dwell together." They knew what the Great Elder meant. They had wondered about their situations. "Would they become like *The Wolf and the Raven*?"

I watched the raven fly back to the forest. A shadowy figure stood at the edge of the wood line. The raven landed on their arm. They went back into the dark forest. I couldn't tell if it was a spirit or a human. If it was a human, they were very powerful for me to miss. I was a little concerned if they were friendly or a powerful enemy. I knew one thing. They were not interested in joining or harming us until we got *The Book of Fall*. I looked back at our camp. I noticed that everyone had gone to their tents to get some sleep. They had much to think about. The only thing that you could hear were the two wolves howling at the full moon.

When you are tired, morning comes too early. When I got up, Nick had already fixed breakfast. After breakfast, I told everyone to wait a few minutes while I look back down the trail where we came from yesterday. I decided to look at a place where we had cut through some brush. When I got there, I saw something strange. The brush had already grown back. It looked like nobody had been here for years. I also looked for any sign of tracks. All of our tracks including whoever was here yesterday was gone. It was as if we had never been here. Nobody would ever be able to follow us. Why were our tracks and brushes put back and cleaned like nobody had been here? My only guess was that whoever is following us doesn't want anyone following either us or them.

When I got back to the group, I didn't tell them anything. All I said was that I didn't see anyone. One Feather said, "We will get there late today. We need to hurry to get there before dark." He set a quick pace. We traveled as fast as we dared. I again put Moses and Nick in back of our line. I asked Lo Ming to guard Antonio as best she could. Naturally, I didn't tell Antonio that Lo Ming was guarding him. I was a little worried that whoever was following us might want Antonio for their own reasons.

We broke for lunch. We wasted no time before getting back on the trail. We were starting to move down into a river valley. It now was the third day of fall. The leaves were starting to turn bright reds and golden yellow. From advantage points on our trail, we could see the whole valley bathed in reds, yellows, green and gold. It was a beautiful sight. It took us another four hours to reach the Drowning River

Little Wolf pointed to some pile of rocks. It didn't look like much from a distance. As we got closer, we could see an outline of a bear. "Nick, that is your bear that you have been looking to find," said Little Wolf. We went to the rock formation. It definitely was the bear formation. We had arrived at the first point in the trail for *The Book of Fall*.

We set up camp. In the center, we put our campfire. One Feather told everyone not to swim or go into the river. The river had a reputation for drowning anyone that went into it. Nick decided to do some fishing for trout. He threw in his line. Suddenly, the line went tight in his hands. Something was pulling very hard on his line. He was starting to be pulled into the river. Moses took out his large knife and quickly cut the fishing string before it could pull Nick into the river. "Gentlemen and ladies, that is why they call this river the Drowning River. It tries to use anything to pull you in and drown you. Do not go near this river!" I told them. It was no surprise when everyone moved their tents and the cooking area about 50 yards from the river.

Lo Ming said, "I know of another river like this in Mongolia. It is said that there are Harpies in the river. They are beautiful women that live on the bottom of the river. They try to get men to follow them into the river. That was one that probably tried to pull Nick into the river. Don't get me wrong, I have nothing against a beautiful woman. I do have something against a beautiful woman that wants to eat me for breakfast."

I told everyone that we are going to double-up on guard duty tonight. Lo Ming and Moses will be on guard the first shift followed by June and One Feather and then Rose and Nick.

Mary and Antonio will take the last shift. The reason that we are using a male and female is obvious. There is one more thing: I have been places where there have been both female and male harpies. You both need to remember that tonight if anyone except one of us comes near you to alert us. We will need to stop them. It will take all of us to push them back into the river. I have made several strong poles to do such a thing. Do not kill any of them or all of them will come out of the water at once. We cannot handle more than two at once.

We ate in silence. I told them about what I had seen in the forest this morning. "Do you think that whoever is following us wants to harm us," asked Little Wolf. Nick said that he could answer part of that question. "Not everything is what it seems. My grandfather told me a story about something like this. He is a great medicine man with our tribe called, **The Others.** He lives in the Southwest desert near Mexico. He has taught me a lot. One thing he taught me was not all things are as they seem.

Here is a story my grandfather taught me long ago when I was your age, Little Wolf. It is called, ***The Big Bear***.

The Crow tribe attacked a Cheyenne camp. A woman escaped with her baby and ran from the Crow. She ran and ran for her baby and her life. She noticed a big Grizzly Bear was following them. She ran faster, but the Grizzly Bear kept following her.

She began to cry because she knew that if the Crow didn't kill her, the bear surely would kill her baby and her. So, she started to run faster again, but the Grizzly Bear kept following her and would not go away!

Finally, she could not run anymore. She fell to the ground in exhaustion. She saw the Grizzly Bear approaching them.

She knew her and her baby were going to die. She cried and begged the Creator to save them.

The Grizzly Bear was 2 steps away from them, when the bear spoke. He said, "Do not be afraid, Cheyenne woman. The Crow Indians will not find you or your baby. I have been following you and covering your tracks the entire time."

So, see Little Wolf, not all is what it seems. The one following us could be a friend or an enemy. We don't know who it is. We have several days before we need to fear whoever it is. Let's hope it is someone like the Grizzly Bear. He is just covering our tracks. If he is, we better hope that he is successful. Too many people want *The Book of Fall* or for us not to be successful. No matter, that is what white men call a rock or a hard place to be. Now get some sleep, Little Wolf. We have a long day tomorrow.

It was about 3 in the morning fog that we heard Mary scream. We ran toward them. There were two Harpies going after Antonio and Mary. Mary had a male harpy against her pole, and Antonio had a female one. Both Harpies were beautiful and handsome. We got our poles and pushed them toward the river. It was very difficult. The wet grass was very slippery. The male Harpy had gotten away from Mary and started to go toward Rose with its sharp teeth glowing. Its eyes told you it was thirsty for blood.

When it was about on Rose, she threw one of her exploding beads. It didn't seem to have any effect on the harpy. Nick tried to stop the Harpy with his pole, but it broke the pole into pieces. I thought we were going to lose this battle or one of us. Out of nowhere came a bright flash of lightning. Both Harpies became suspended into the air about 15 feet above us. Something moved the Harpies toward the river. We could not see what happened next because of the low fog except we could hear two splashes of water.

The Harpies were gone. I told everyone to get by the campfire and build it up. I would make us some torches if needed. The fire would keep the Harpies away for the rest of the night. We would be pulling out first thing in the morning when we could see. Nobody got any more sleep before morning light. Was it a curse or luck to have someone watching us? That thought was on everyone's mind. We only hoped that, whoever it was, was a friend. Someone so powerful would be hard to beat.

John asked Antonio who the next passage belonged to. Antonio surprised him by saying one word, "You."

This passage had surprised Antonio. He hadn't expected a passage for him. Antonio had given him a passage several days ago. John told the others what the passage said.

Darkness Will Come in the Middle of the Day

Wait to see at the lagoon
Grandfather sun behind grandmother moon
Darkness will come in the middle of the day
Nowhere to run, no words to say

You will not hear a sound
No animals will be around
You must look to yourself
In the end, it's all you have left

You will find yourself alone
Everything you know is suddenly gone
What's left is all in your mind
Everything you know is left behind

You must find a way of survival
You must find a way of renewal
Think before anything you do
My brother, it is up to you

The silence will be all you hear
The loneliness will be all you fear
Nowhere to run, no words to say
Darkness will come in the middle of the day

"This passage is more about our destination than a direction to go. It's about a lake. When we arrive at a certain lake, we will need to wait until there is an eclipse which will be at midday. That's what Darkness will come in the middle of the day means: an eclipse. There are some other clues about this place. Silence is all you hear means a cave. Everything is dark and there is nothing in a cave. This means that we must find the cave before the eclipse before noon on that day. If we do the cave will open for us. I know where we are going. There is a legend of a cave full of riches. This cave is called The Cave of lost Treasures. If you have something that you want, it will appear in the cave. The only problem is that if you take anything out of the cave you cannot ever go back. *The Book of Fall* must be in that cave. "You must think before anything you do." Every one of us will be tempted by something that you have always wanted. If you can think it, it will be somewhere in the main part of the cave. That is all I can tell you," said John.

Antonio said that Moses was next. His passage was called "The Music of Our Land." Moses said that it went like this:

74

The Music of Our Land

If you try to find
Something beyond your mind
You will come to understand
If you listen to the music of the land

Listen to the drops of rain that fall
Listen to the crows that caw
Listen to the song of the wind
Listen to the boughs that bend

Listen to the croak of a frog
Listen to the bark of a dog
Listen to the softness of a horse's sigh
Listen to the pain of a river's cry

Listen to the song of a bird
Listen to all you have heard
Then you will begin to understand
The way to our unknown land

Little brother, only you can hear
You'll know our spirits are near
Little brother, only you can understand
The meaning in the music of our Land

Moses said, "We must find a waterfall. That's the meaning of drops of rain that fall. We must listen to nature. First, we must listen to the crows that caw and follow them. Then we must follow the direction of the wind until we heard the branches of pine bending and swaying. The next direction we must go is where there are sounds of frogs. When we hear a bark of a dog, we will be close to the Valley of the Horses. When we get to the Valley of Horses, we will go in the direction of the roar of rapids, that's the pain of the river's cry. Finally, when we hear the songbirds, we will know that we have arrived at the point where we will hear all types of the sounds of nature. This will be the point to start another passage.

One Feather said he had heard of the Valley of Horses. It is a sacred valley that only the bravest can go. The horses are very wild. If the horses feel that you are there for selfish reasons, they will stampede and try to run you over. The valley is hidden, and you must be invited there. We must go as quietly as possible in order to hear the sounds of nature.   I put Moses in the lead. This was going to be a test of memory and physical endurance for Moses.

I asked if anyone knew when the eclipse would happen. Moses spoke up, "Judging by the restlessness of the animals around here, I would say in about three days. Rose said, "I looked at the stars and planets. Moses is right. The moon will be coming up in the daylight by the way it is traveling at night. We need to hurry.

We stood still for a few moments. Birds could be heard in the distance. Moses told everyone to wait. After about five minutes, a crow flew overhead. It was heading North. Moses signaled for everyone not to move. Soon you could hear several crows calling to the Southwest. Moses turned around and pointed to the Southwest. We followed Moses in that direction.

The terrain was steep and rocky. Moses found a faint trail that hadn't been traveled on for years. There were loose and sharp rocks with small bushes that had sharp thorns on their branches growing in the trail. Moses told everyone to be careful. The thorns of the small bushes would give you a bad wound if you got cut by them. He thought that this was one reason that this path was chosen by the old medicine man that hid the books.

The going was very slow because of the thorny bushes. We reached a top of a small mountain in two hours. The caw of the crows had stopped. The view from the mountain was beautiful. You could see the mountain ranges to the South and West of us. They were bright with gold, red, and brown leaves. The green needles of pine trees contrasted with the bright hardwood colors. We decided to take a rest here for a few minutes to catch our breath. The climb had been difficult. Everyone sat down on a rock or the grass to rest. I worried a little about Moses. He had not completely recovered for his earlier injuries. I could tell he was having a hard time leading us.

Mary went over to Moses and gave him some pills to take. She told him it would ease the pain of his sore muscles. Lo Ming had been watching him closely. She whispered in his ear to go slow and not to hurry. She knew that Moses would not listen. Moses was too proud to let on he was having trouble.

Moses got up. He pointed to the East. We looked at him as to why he pointed in that direction. In a few moments, we knew why. We were hit by a gust of wind from the West. Moses had sensed the wind coming. We got up and started down the east side of the mountain. It was difficult. Nick said he always thought going down a mountain was harder than going up. I could see people nodded their heads to that. We traveled down the mountain. When we reached the base of the mountain, Moses stopped. He pointed to several large pine trees. The branches and pine needles were swaying in the wind. We waited patiently until Moses started walking to the Northeast. We soon heard frogs croaking in that direction. We knew that water was near. The brush was thick, and the ground was wet from springs coming out of the mountain base. As we neared a large spring, several very large bullfrogs jumped into the water.

We must have startled them. This was the end of the croaking of the frogs. We stopped to rest and have a snack. We were all getting pretty tired. Nick handed out some homemade health bars he had made.

You could see through the trees that the forest was ending. Light was shining through the leaves about two hundred yards ahead. Moses jumped up and told everyone we had to go quickly. He started in the direction where the forest was ending. The bark of many animals could be heard. June and I had heard that sound many times on the prairie. It was the sound of prairie dogs. That indicated to us that a large valley was probably near.

As we cleared the last of the trees of the forest, ahead of us was a grassy valley. The bark of the prairie dogs stopped as we reached the beginning of the valley. One Feather moved up to stop Moses. One Feather signaled us to stop. In the distance, we could hear the thunder of horses' hoofs. There had to be at least a hundred or more of them. They were coming right toward us.

One Feather signed to tell us not to move until the horses got here. He and Moses would talk to the herd's leader. It wasn't long before we saw the herd in the distance. At the front of the herd of mustangs was a large spotted light brown mustang stallion. Both One Feather and Moses held up their hands in a sign of peace. The leader stopped the herd. He trotted up to One Feather and Moses. One Feather whispered something to the stallion. The stallion nodded his head. Moses placed his hand on his head. They seemed to be communicating with each other.

The herd behind the stallion was getting restless. The leader had to turn his head several times to make sure they wouldn't come any closer. The leader soon returned to the herd. Moses told us to not be afraid. The leader would have several of the others of his herd come over to us. We were not to move. They would be checking to see if our hearts were pure enough to go on to their valley. If anyone of us showed signs of not being pure in our mission, they would stomp them to death. Moses had a smile on his face. I wondered if Moses was joking or telling us the truth. Moses did have a funny sense of humor.

Several large stallions moved toward us. Each horse had picked one of us to check out. I saw Antonio sweating a little. He was not the only one. Mary and Lo Ming seemed to be very concerned. I could see that the stallion that was checking out Antonio was not happy with him. He took his large head and knocked Antonio to the ground. He raised his large front hoof and struck at Antonio. Antonio did not move. The horse's hoof missed him by a fraction of an inch. I had to give Antonio credit. He had nerves of steel. If Antonio had moved, the horse would have killed him.

Everyone else seemed to pass the test. However, I saw something that worried me. It seemed that the horses that checked out Mary and Lo Ming were not too happy with them. They knocked them down. They took their heads and rolled them around in the grass. Mary and Lo Ming just let them do it. The horses seemed to like playing with them. When Mary and Lo Ming smiled at them, they stopped and went back to the herd. When they got there, they went up to the leader and whispered something in his ear.

After a few minutes, the leader came back and went up to me. He put his head on my head. His mind told me, "He knew I was the leader of this group. There are legends about a man in a hat with a seven on it." Visions came to me. He was telling me not to trust everything about those two women that his stallions had knocked down in the grass. They were not as true as the others, but he would let them pass. It was up to me to find out why.

The man, Antonio, was one to watch but he would be loyal to you.

The lead stallion knew that I would need everyone to find what we were looking for. He knew the hope of his herd's future depended on us being successful. To save time, he would let us ride on his stallions' backs. The waterfall that Moses was seeking was about an hour from here. It would be getting close to dark soon. We could camp there for the night. The songbirds would be out in the morning. Moses could find them then.

With the help of the herd, we got to the waterfalls just before dark. The rapids in the river was loud. As we dismounted the stallions, the leader came up to me. He put his head on mine once again. I could clearly hear his thoughts. "Be careful, John, there is danger near. My scout horses know that you are being followed by several dangerous creatures. They are not of this world. They will probably not harm you until you get *The Book of Fall.* The last time we saw such creatures was when a great Medicine Man was carrying a book to hide. He told us that the creatures would kill anyone that was successful in finding the book he was carrying. He said it in such a way that it was for us to warn anyone looking for the book he was carrying. May your journey be safe, and you live long. There is one more thing. There is a legend that your son will be the one that frees *The Book of Winter,* if his mother doesn't kill you first." I swore that the leader of the herd smiled at me as he ran off to take his herd south.

We made camp and gathered firewood for the night. Rose and I went to the river and caught some fine trout for supper. Mary and Nick started the campfire while June and One Feather tried to find some other food. It didn't take long for them to find some wild mushrooms, onions and sweet potatoes. They also found some asparagus. Lo Ming had made Moses and her tents together. She knew by the way Moses was acting that Moses had worn himself out. She made him a soft bed of grass and leaves and covered it with a blanket. She had him lie down and rest while supper was being fixed. Moses was fast asleep in a few minutes.

The smell of the food being cooked was a welcome change. It had been a while since they had this much food to eat. Lo Ming took a plate of food to Moses. It took some doing to wake Moses up. Moses wolfed the food down like he hadn't eaten for weeks. Lo Ming had made some special tea with herbs she had brought from back home. Moses drank the hot tea. He started to say something but fell to sleep in seconds after drinking it. "Now Moses, my love, you need to rest. The potion I gave you should help you sleep and get better by morning," she said to his sleeping body.

After supper, we gathered by the campfire. It was a beautiful night. The sky was filled with stars. The moon was almost full. Its color was a bright red. Nick looked at me, "Why don't you tell them what the stallion told you, John?" "What do you mean," I asked. "We have a group of something following us. They have been keeping about two miles behind us for the last few days. I sense they are not people. They are some sort of creatures. Who are they?" he asked me. The rest of our group leaned in to hear what I had to say.

"All I know is what the stallion leader told me. He said that the Medicine Man that hid *The Book of Fall* had creatures with him to protect the book if it was found. He said that we would have no problems with them until we actually find the book. By the way he told me, I feel that he is right. He said these creatures were something not of this world. I didn't know about them until the stallion leader told me," I replied. Nick replied back, "I thought you did. You are right. They seemed more interested in following us. I could tell by the way they took their time in not getting too close to us. I suggest that we get some good sleep tonight. I wish we had Midnight and Snow with us. They could stand watch for us."

As if on cue, we heard the howl of two wolves near the tree line. Snow and Midnight came running toward us. One Feather and June grabbed them into their arms. June looked at Nick, "Now you know the secret. Just wish for them and they will come especially if it is to protect someone they love." Nick went over and petted both of them. "Will you stand guard tonight so we can get some sleep?" he asked them. They answered by licking his face. Everyone laughed at Nick. The two wolves ran off into the night. Nick said, "All they had to do was nod or howl. They didn't have to lick me." Little Wolf seemed to laugh the hardest at Nick.

We soon went to our tents to get some sleep. I had Little Wolf stay with me in my tent. I told Little Wolf before we went to sleep to stay close to Mary if we had any problems. "I want you to protect Mary. She will protect you. Never worry about me. I am expendable. Everyone else here is needed to get the books. Remember that: promise me that you will protect yourself and the others," I commanded him. Reluctantly, he replied, "Yes."

Chapter VI
Will they find the book?
Will they survive?

It was just getting light when Nick started cooking breakfast. He heard a growl behind him. It was Snow and Midnight. "I know what you want. You want some breakfast." Nick took out some dried jerky and tossed to each of them. They caught it in mid-air and ran off into the woods. He heard June say behind him, "Now you will never get rid of them. They will

82

expect this every day." "They earned it. I didn't want to be licked by them this early in the morning," he laughed.

We ate breakfast and gathered up camp. Moses had everyone wait while he listened. To the North of us, we could hear the song of songbirds. He told everyone to follow him. After traveling upriver for about a mile, we reached a spot where the trees and bushes were filled with hundreds of songbirds. As the birds sang, other animals joined in. You could hear the bark of the groundhogs, the howl of coyotes and wolves, buzzing of bees, chatter of squirrels, a few roars of bears and mountain lions along with many other animals. It was nature's wonderful chorus of music. We listened until the music stopped. The valley became silent again.

Antonio turned to June. "It's now your turn June to lead. What was your passage that I gave to you?" June recited it to everyone. It's called:

A Tree Without a Leaf

Feel the heat of grandfather sun
Remember all that you've done
Watch the light of grandmother moon
The moving shadow of a raccoon

Hear the whisper of the wind
Remember how it's always been
Watch in the middle of a shower
The gentle swaying of a flower

See without opening your eyes
Remember where an eagle flies
Watch in the middle of a storm
The memory of a baby being born

Touch the rock that doesn't feel
Remember all that you thought real
Watch as the eagle flies bye
The rock begins to cry

Look for a tree without a leaf
Remember when you had your belief
It may not all be so
Hey yi, hey yi, hey yi, yo

"We will need to go East to face the hot sun," June said. June was in the lead with One Feather following her. I put Nick last in the line. Lo Ming and Moses were just ahead of Nick with the rest of us in the middle. Nick knew why he was last. He was to make sure we didn't get any unwanted visitors.

June stopped about an hour into the march. She pointed to the pale moon to the Southeast of us. "My tribe calls the pale moon during the light of day, Grandmother's moon because it is grey like a grandmother's hair. We need to go Southeast and follow it."

We went for about another hour when June stopped again. She pointed at a mountain to the South of us. A shadow of the cloud was making a dark figure on a mountain. The figure looked like a raccoon. We started heading that direction. Another hour passed before June stopped again. They wind had picked up. It started to rain. It was just a shower. June had everyone stop. She closed her eyes. In her mind, she saw an eagle. She remembered that the last time she saw an eagle fly, it was going Northwest. She didn't have to say anything as she headed Northwest.

I remembered the phrase about a rock that doesn't feel. I knew what that was. It was a touchstone. That's a black crystal that tells the purity of gold or silver. When we came across a layer of black crystal on a cliff, I told June to stop. She said she was about to stop, but she had to find a place where the rock was crying. After a few feet, she pointed to the layer of black crystal that had water running out of it. She stopped and looked high above the cliff. Nearly two hundred feet above us was a large pine tree about 50 feet tall. "That's where we must go, a tree without a leaf."

It took us 30 minutes to climb the cliff to get to the pine tree. Antonio looked at Lo Ming and said, "It's your turn to lead." Lo Ming recited her passage.

The Secret to the Way to Our Land

I see said grandmother moon
Far beyond the deep lagoon
I hear said grandfather sun
Far beyond where the buffalo run

Look up to Father sky
Watch for the eagle to fly
Look up to Mother Earth
Watch for the signs in the dirt

Look up to the Upper World
Watch for the clouds to swirl
Look down to the Lower World
Watch for the leaves to twirl

Look for the shooting star
It is the center of where you are
Look ahead and look behind
Look inside and outside of your mind

When you find the tiger eye
When the sky begins to cry
You will know and understand
The secret to the way to our land

"I believe that when we finish my passage, we will be close to the place where the book is at. That's why it's called: ***The Secret to the Way to our Land***," stated Lo Ming. Lo Ming pointed toward the pale grandmother moon. "We must go toward the lagoon or lake over there. Then we must follow a buffalo trail west toward grandfather sun which is the setting sun going down in the west. We must hurry. We have only two days to get there before the eclipse." We headed due South toward the lagoon. It would take us most of the day to get to the lagoon. We had the better part of the day left. We didn't waste any time. We hiked as fast as possible.

It was about 3 o'clock when we found the lagoon. The sun was started to head due west to set. We found a buffalo trail to follow. It made traveling faster. The trail was like a road. It was about 10 feet wide and beaten down smooth.

Lo Ming was always looking toward the sky. She fell down a few times by not watching where she was going. She stopped and pointed toward the sky. An eagle flew directly across the trail in front of us. Lo Ming ran to where the shadow of the eagle crossed the buffalo trail. In that area was the sign of an arrow in the dirt. The arrow pointed Northwest. There was a side trail that went Northwest. Lo Ming followed that with us behind her.

The trail became steeper. Soon we were near the top of a tall mountain. The wind was starting to blow stronger. Lo Ming stopped and looked at the top of the mountain. A cloud of fog was swirling around it by the strong wind. She turned around and looked down at the valley below. A dust devil had formed in the valley below twirling leaves all around. "We must camp here and watch for a shooting star tonight. When we see a shooting star. Then we should look in that direction. It will storm later tonight. In the storm, lightning will light up the sky. Looking in the direction of the shooting star, we will need to see a tiger's eye. Whatever that is, it will look like the Tigers Eye gemstone in some formation in the distance. That is where the book lies," she said.

We didn't pitch our tents. We decided to wait until we saw the shooting star first. We would then pitch one large tent using several of our tents and wait out the storm that was to come. Night falls quickly in the mountains. In the distance we could see a large storm approaching. There was no moon because the storm blotted it out. We were about to give it up because the storm was so near. We all froze. The biggest shooting star, we had ever seen came crashing down to our South. It hit the side of a lake glowing in the dark. We watched it glow a bright yellow and gold with some red. The rain soon followed. We didn't have time to put the tents together. We just threw them over us to protect us from the hard rain.

Lo Ming yelled that she saw the Tiger's Eye in the distance. She pointed in the direction of the shooting star. It was the meteor. The meteor was still glowing. The rain was distorting the light coming from it. It looked like a Tiger's Eye from this distance. "There is where the book lies. It is near there. I can barely make out a lake near it when the lightning flashes. She took an arrow from Mary's pack and pointed it directly at the meteor. That is the direction we will go tomorrow," she stated.

It rained and stormed most of the night. We had to wait until morning light to go back down the trail. It was too slippery to do at night. We started down the trail at light. June and One Feather led the way. One Feather had studied the direction of the meteor. He said that he knew where to go. He had been there before with the Red Woman. The lake was a sacred place. Nobody was allowed there unless accompanied by a Medicine Woman or Man. One Feather said that it would take us most of the day to get there. We had to hurry. Tomorrow was the eclipse.

Nick gave us the last of his health bars to eat on the way. We half ran and hiked at the fastest pace we could. Hours passed quickly. We cut our way through thick brush. It was about two hours till dark when we got to the meteor. The lake was just behind it.

Antonio looked at Mary. It is your turn to find the cave or whatever. Mary recited her passage.

The Little Bird in the Nest

I saw a little bird in the nest
Abandoned by all the rest
He cried out his mama's name
But his mama never came

I said little bird, I'm just like you
I don't know what to do
I'm scared and all alone
Everyone else has already gone

I watched as he chirped to the sky
I knew that he was too scared to fly
It was a long way to the ground
There were no other birds around

I heard his cries for another bird
I knew his cries would not be heard
Just like I cried for you today
There was nothing left to say

I felt the little bird's pain
I knew his cries were all in vain
Left alone by all the rest
I'm like that little bird in a nest

Mary looked at Little Wolf. "This passage is about you. You were left with Red Woman. I know you cried because you missed your mother. You were like a little bird in a nest. I once cried for a son that I thought was dead. Where did you go when you dealt with being lonely, Little Wolf?" Mary asked. Little Wolf thought a while. "I would climb high up into a tall tree. Then I would come down and play in a sandy area by a spring. I wanted to be a bird, but I didn't try to fly. I would make sculptures of birds with clay and sand. I would build a nest of sand around it. Look over there, Mary, see that sand. It looks much like the nest I would build in the sand by my home," said Little Wolf.

Mary walked over to where Little Wolf pointed. She motioned all of us to come and look. When we got there, we saw a hole in the ground. That hole had been uncovered by the meteor. There was a little bird trapped in the sand in the hole. Little Wolf helped pull it out of the hole. We heard cries of another bird. Little Wolf put the little bird on the sand, and it flew away toward the bird's mother in the sky. "I could feel the little bird's pain. I am glad that I could help it. I was once like that little bird in the nest trapped and my cries at night were in vain." Mary went over to Little Wolf and pulled him close to her. She hugged him like she would never let him go. Little Wolf hugged her back. He felt her love for him. He would never cry in vain again.

If it wasn't for the tears in our eyes, we would all be happy. We had found the cave. We only had to wait until noon tomorrow for the eclipse to open it. Antonio looked at Rose.

Rose, your passage will be important tomorrow. You will have to solve the riddle of your passage for us to find the book in the cave. You need to study it tonight. Finding the book in the cave will be up to you. Nick turned around. We will have to post a guard with our wolves tonight. I can sense the creatures are near us and watching us. If we return from the cave tomorrow, I can assure you, we will be in a fight for our lives.

We set up our campsite with our tents in a semi-circle facing away from the lake. I could see that everyone was examining their weapons. They were making sure that the weapons were in working conditions. Rose had put together her bags of exploding beads. Antonio had his wand. He also had a several throwing knives. He said that he thought they would come in handy. Moses had his whip and large bowie knife. Lo Ming had her walking stick and had pulled out a small Chinese sword. Mary had her bow and arrows. June had her tomahawk, bow and arrows. Nick said that he was ready. He had his trusted iron frying pan. Everyone laughed at Nick. He smiled because he knew that he could change the frying pan into a long sword. They knew that Nick had his K-Bar Military fighting knife at his side. Everyone looked at me. I pulled out my 50 cal. Hawken Rifle. They knew I always carried my bowie knife.

We ate in silence. I gave everyone the times of the guard duty shifts. One Feather and June took the first two-hour watch. One Feather always carried his bow and arrow. I had made that for him. It took a strong man to pull the string back on it. I had made him some arrows with special steel arrow heads. They could penetrate the thickest hide or bullet proof vest.

Little Wolf asked if he could have a weapon. Mary told him that she had something special for him. She went in her tent and came back with a package. Little Wolf tore open the package. In it was a beautiful hunting knife. It was engraved in gold with a wolf howling at the moon. The handle was black gemstone that was not smooth so it wouldn't slip out of your hand. There were two green and blue gems on the bottom of each side of the handle. It was painful to see. I remembered that knife from long ago.

"Little Wolf, a special man in my past gave this to me. He left a note in the package that he sent me. It said: *"**Give this to your son or daughter when they become of age. It will protect them.**"* I don't remember anything about him. I can't remember my past. If it wasn't for the note and letter inside the package, I wouldn't know that much. I do know one thing. I will always treat you as a son. It is yours to keep. You are a man." Tears were running down Mary's face. She turned and ran back to her tent.

I didn't give Mary guard duty. She had too much on her mind. Little Wolf asked me one question, "Mary is my mother, isn't she?" I looked down on him. The only thing I could do was say, "Yes." Little Wolf replied, "I knew it from the moment I saw her. A child always knows his mother."

The night passed without any problems. We ate breakfast. I had everyone pack up their tents and packs. We put our packs near a large sand dune. I had Nick and Antonio cover them. I didn't want the creatures destroying our packs. It was a long way back to Eagle Mountain. The only things we carried were our weapons and water. The only thing left was to wait until the Eclipse.

We watched the waves come to shore on the lake. It was a clear day. The fall sun was hot on our backs as we looked at the blue lake. A few clouds moved across the skyline. The birds and other wildlife seemed restless. They could sense something was going to happen.

Rose told everyone that her passage was a riddle. It would be better if everyone knew what it said. "Eight minds are better

than one. You may see something I have not in the passage."
She recited her passage very slowly and carefully to us.

Maybe It's Not What It Seems to Be

Time is a circle spinning around
Down is up, Up is down
Everything you think you see
May not be What it seems to be

West is East, East is West
Maybe it's just a test
Everything you think is near
May not even be here

Earth is water, Water is Earth
Birth is death, Death is birth
Everything you think you feel
May not even be real

High is low, Low is high
Maybe you should ask why
Everything you think you know
May not even be so

Birds are us, We are birds
Hear the meaning of our words
Oh, mother earth, father sky
Hey, yi, Hey, yi, Hey, yi, Hi

Antonio whistled. "When we get in the cave, Rose must lead.
Remember, do not take anything from the cave. If you do, we
will all be doomed to die in the cave. You will see the wonders

of the world. Gold and treasures beyond anything you will ever see. It will be tempting to take something."

The Eclipse started exactly on time. It was high noon. As the sun was starting to be covered, the hole in the sand became bigger. Rose told us not to go too close to the hole. "Remember: **Down is up**." You could see a door opening in the hole. "Wait don't move. It is a trap," she shouted. The longer we waited, the larger the hole got. Soon it looked like a cave. When Nick started to jump in, Antonio grabbed him. Immediately, the hole caved in with sand filling it. The ground shook. From the sand and ground, a tunnel moved up from beneath the sand. A large entrance appeared with a large stone door.

There were four doorknobs on the stone door much like the four directions of the compass. One was on top with two on each side and one on bottom of the door. **"West is East, East is West"** Rose said. Rose went over and carefully turned both the doorknobs in the middle of the door and the same time. Then she jumped back. The heavy stone door fell crashing down where she had been standing. **"Up is Down,"** she said.

We followed Rose inside the entrance to the cave. We had made torches, but they were not needed. Torches on the walls were already lit. The main hall was covered with priceless jewels and diamonds. This magnified the light of the torches. We slowly moved down the hallway. There were large rooms on both sides of the hallway filled with gold coins and treasure. Lo Ming stopped for a few moments. She pointed out a gold sword on top of a pile of gold coins. "That is the missing sword of Julius Caesar, and that is the missing scepter of Alexander the Great." She didn't have to say anything more. Every lost treasure you could imagine was here. We reached the final room of the hallway.

"Everything you think is near
  May not even be here"

Rose recited. "Don't touch anything. The things we see are
not real. It's from your imagination. They are things you
would like to have or find. There is more to this puzzle. Turn
around and look down the hallway. I know that this sounds
strange. I want you to think about the world we know, of its
oceans and islands, of life and death, no matter how painful it
is.

"Earth is water, Water is Earth
  Birth is death, Death is birth" She recited to us.

All the treasures disappeared in the rooms. The rooms started
to fill with visions. Each room had a vision from each one of
us. We saw how each of us envisioned the world and its oceans
and land. We also saw how we viewed life and death. That
was the most painful visions of all.

"Everything you think you feel
  May not even be real," Rose recited.

"Stop thinking and feeling about these things or you will go
mad with the pain."
Think about these lines, they will help you return. I know they
are nonsense.

'High is low, Low is high
  Maybe you should ask why
  Everything you think you know
  May not even be so"

The visions in the rooms disappeared at once. Our painful
memories and emotions were lifted from us. We felt free of the
things that had haunted many of us for years. The only thing in
front of us was an empty hallway. The jewels and diamonds
were gone. Only the torches on the walls remained.

  "Now we come to the hardest part. Everyone must recite the
last lines of the passage with me. You must pay attention to the

last word. The last word will reveal *The Book of Fall.* Look
where the last word says. Now we start:

Birds are us, We are birds
Hear the meaning of our words
Oh, mother earth, father sky
Hey, yi, Hey, yi, Hey, yi, Hi

   As we said the words, each one of us saw a vision of our
favorite bird. Cardinals, eagles, songbirds and many other birds
flew down the hallway. When we came to the last word "Hi,"
all the birds stopped and flew into the center of the hallway's
ceiling and formed a leather and jewel covered book attached to
the ceiling. We had all looked at the ceiling at the same time.
We knew that we had found *The Book of Fall*.
   Rose yelled for everyone to run for the door. Antonio jumped
up and pulled down the book from the ceiling. He put in under
his shirt behind his back. Sand was leaking down from above
us. Antonio was the last one out of the door. The cave was
sinking into the sand. In seconds, everything was gone.
   Little Wolf pointed in the direction of the valley. In front of
us were ten ugly creatures. They looked like half man-half ape.
They were about 7 foot tall. Thick black hair covered their
bodies. Animal skins covered their mid-sections. They all had
long swords in both hands. There was blood in their eyes.
They were not here for the fun of it.
   I had everyone line up in a horizontal line to face them. I
looked to see if they had a leader. If they had one, just maybe I
could talk to them. They had to be intelligent to have lived this
long. They didn't attack us while we were searching for the
book. Something here didn't add up. Why were they waiting?
They had the superior numbers and strength.

Before I could stop him, Little Wolf walked out in front of us. One creature walked toward him. I saw Mary point her arrow at the creature in front of Little Wolf. Little Wolf held up his hand and started to speak in sign language to the creature. To our surprise, the creature spoke back to Little Wolf in sign.

We waited as Little Wolf and the creature spoke to each other for several minutes. Little Wolf turned and spoke in sign to us. The lead creature turned to speak in sign to his group. Little Wolf took out his knife that Mary had given him and walked to the middle of the group of creatures. The lead creature held out his arm. Little Wolf did the same. Little Wolf cut his arm until it bled. The lead creature did the same. Each placed the arms together and shook their arms together. All the creatures in front of us held up their swords and bowed at the waist toward Little Wolf. We did the same toward them. Like it or not, we now were all blood brothers.

Little Wolf moved back to our line. He took out his knife and pointed it at the creatures. A flash of lightning hit each creature in front of us. They all fell down onto the sand. It looked like they were all dead. Little Wolf motioned in sign to stay where we were. After several minutes, the creatures started to shake and moan. As they were shaking on the ground, they started to mutate into another form. The lead creature was the first to stand up. Then the others followed one by one. In front of us were 10 Indian braves. They were men again. They ran to us to greet us.

Their leader explained that the great Medicine Man had transformed them into creatures to guard *The Book of Fall*. At first, they thought they were performing a great service to **The Land of Eagle Feathers.** After many years, they realized that the Medicine Man had tricked them. They had fought several people who had tried to find the book. They had done many things they were not proud of protecting it. They did their duty.

When the smallest of our group went out to talk to them, they couldn't fight him. Little Wolf had told them enough blood had been shed over the books. It was time for them to go home. Little Wolf had told them that the only way to save this land was to find *The Book of Winter*. Little Wolf was a great warrior to face so many. We had to take the word of the great warrior.

I told them that their families were long gone. They said that they knew. It was time for them to go home to their great grandchildren. We gave them our tents to make clothing from and left to go back home ourselves. Later that night at our campsite, we asked why Little Wolf did what he did? Little Wolf only answered, "My Grandmother taught me well. Antonio was not the only one that could read ancient writings. I have many talents. You just never asked."

Chapter VII
Angela Returns to Houston:
Will she be able to survive?

Angela made it through the tunnel out of The Land of the Eagle Feathers without much trouble. She had been surprised to see that someone had left open the tunnel's entrance. It was like someone had been expecting her. She knew the walk back to Eagle Train Station would take her several days. She had a bad feeling and needed to get to Houston as quickly as possible. She had traveled down the trail about a mile when she saw two horses and a mule in the middle of the trail. One of the horses was a fine, black stallion with a silver trimmed saddle. There was an old brown hound dog with them.

The old hound dog came running toward her. The old hound stopped a few feet in front of her. On its collar was a note. She reached over and took the note from its collar. The note said,

"I am here to help you. I have an extra horse, food and clothing. Do not worry, I'm the old man from the Train Station. Come on down and get some food." Angela couldn't wait to get some food and fresh clothes. She had been suspicious for years about who the old man was. How did he know she would be here? Right now, she didn't care. Any help is better than none.

The old man was waiting in the shade of a boulder near the horses. "Well now, I see that you made it out okay. I thought you would. Your great grandfather had taught you well. There's a good spring two miles down the trail. We can stop there and fix you some food. You could use a good bath in the spring before going down the mountain. There will be a train waiting to get you back to Houston. I am pretty sure that's where you are going. David needs to see you. He was worried about you. I think he was more worried about himself. But David was always that way. Even when he was just a little pup. Now get on the brown mare and let's get going." Angela was too stunned to say anything. She was too tired to anyway.

The old man told Angela to unsaddle the horses and mule. They had reached the clearing in the forest that had a warm spring. While she was doing that, he fixed her a hot meal. Eggs, bacon and coffee with some biscuits and blackberry jam was what was on the menu today. The old man told her sit over on a log near the campfire. He dished up both of them a large plateful of food and handed her a cup of hot black coffee. She hadn't tasted a cup of coffee for months. When she tasted her food, she was surprised. This old man could cook. It was when she tasted the coffee, she couldn't believe it. This coffee was very expensive. It was her favorite. "How do you like your coffee? I put some honey in it for sweetness. I think you like it that way," the old man asked.

"How did he know about the coffee and honey?" she asked. "Well child, I know about a lot of things. The old hound dog told me. When you get through eating, you can take a bath in warm springs down there. You look like you need it. There's some shampoo and soap in the bag with some clothes for you. I brought you some clothes to change into. I suggest you burn the clothes you have on. They deserve a proper burial," he laughed.

Angela didn't ask the old man any more questions. She knew he wouldn't answer them anyway. In all the years she knew him, he never talked about himself. He did say one thing that bothered her before he left to go up the mountain. "I'll leave you some food and my black stallion to take you back to the train station. When you get there, let him loose, and he will come back to me. I must wait up here for another lost soul to come back."

Angela went to the warm spring. She laughed when she took out the shampoo and soap from the small bag. The shampoo and soap were what she always used. She settled herself down in the warm water. It felt so relaxing. Her thoughts turned to the trouble that was coming. David would have so many questions that she would need to find good answers. He was ruthless. She didn't know how to tell him about her relationship with **The Land of the Eagle Feathers**. She would take the chance and tell him the truth. Red Woman was another problem for her. She did have one ace in the hole. She might have to use it to save her life.

After her bath, she changed into the clothes the old man brought. The black leather pants and silk shirt fit her perfectly. She took her time in combing her hair. The comb had been carved out of walnut and had a dark stain on it. The old man sure could carve. Still the old man couldn't know her size for the clothing. Only a woman would know that.

She went back to the campsite. The fire was now just coals. She took her old clothes and threw them on the fire. She watched them burn. She put on a blue wind breaker that was in the clothes bag. As she watched the clothes burn, she noticed something. There was another set of tracks on the ground around the campfire. She followed them. The footprint had to be a woman's footprint. They started as a dog's paw print. The dog's print vanished, and a woman's footprint began. Then the woman's footprint vanished, and a dog's paw print began. Could it be? She tossed that thought from her mind. She put such thoughts out of her mind. She extinguished the fire and saddled the black stallion. It would take her a full day and all night to get to the train station. It was a great feeling to have such a powerful horse under her.

David was being asked a lot of questions about where Angela was. He knew that he could only make up so many excuses. He had been to the hospital to check on the progress of Shanna. She was in rehab for her wounds. She had been making good progress. Nick's grandparents were still there. They would be taking Shanna back to their place in a few days. He knew Nick's grandparents did not like him. He knew the reason why. They had a truce of some sorts. Only because they knew he had to protect her. She had saved his life twice.

He had a lot of respect for Shanna. She was not only beautiful. She was tough as nails. She was smart, but not too smart. It was no wonder that Angela and Shanna were somehow friends. They were like two peas in a pod. He laughed at himself. Why were all the women around him so dangerous? Perhaps it was that he liked it that way. Everyone knows the female is the most dangerous animal in the universe. He did like to live on the edge. It wasn't always that way.

It was about midnight when something woke up Shanna in her hospital room. It was semi-dark. She felt her before she saw her. Angela was sitting in the hospital chair beside her. "I told you to protect Antonio, not to get yourself killed," Angela smiled at Shanna. Shanna replied, "Antonio is a good-looking man. I imagine he has a lot of men wanting to kill him. Too bad it was two females that wanted him dead." "You figured it out. You had plenty of time to do that lying here," Angela stated.

"I guess you saved One Feather and Moses or you wouldn't be here. Is Nick alright?" Shanna asked. "Mary had to take care of him for a time, but he is fine. That's a long story, I will tell you more later. Thank You for saving Antonio, Shanna." "It's funny how things work out, Angela. If I hadn't got hurt, Nick wouldn't have realized that he loved me?" said Shanna with a tear in her eye. "And if you hadn't told Antonio you promised me to protect him, he wouldn't have told me the same thing, Shanna," Angela said as she leaned over and kissed Shanna on her forehead.

Shanna smiled, "There is one thing more. We are somewhat tied together by Antonio. I have his blood in my veins. He gave me his blood. He insisted on giving me his blood for the transfusions I needed." "Well, at least, he did something right. Why is it that women have to protect men?" said Angela. "It's because men are so dumb," Shanna replied as Angela left her room.

The next morning, Angela walked straight into David's office. David started to say something. Angela wouldn't let him talk. "Why did you let Raven and Benita get to Antonio? I thought you knew better," Angela asked. David didn't like Angela's attitude. "Well now, Angela, you have explaining to do yourself. You have been holding out on me. How did you get into **The Land of the Eagle Feathers?**" David replied.

"I see it's show and tell time," said Angela. "Let's say I have a relative in high places. You are not the only one. I saw how

101

you looked at the Red Woman. A woman knows that look. You still care for her after all these years. I thought you said your wife was dead." David was losing his patience. He thought he had better calm down. He wasn't going to play Angela's game. In a calm voice he asked Angela about One Feather and Moses. "They are doing fine. The last I know before leaving was they were all together going about finding *The Book of Fall.* I predict they should be here in a couple of weeks or less. One thing you should know was that the Red Woman saved Moses' life. She is sure some woman, but you know that already."

"Sometimes, Angela. I think you are more trouble than you are worth," David said with sarcasm. "I know you don't mean that at all. I have brought in many millions to the organization through the years. I have done your dirty work. I have watched you get more and more deeper into this rotten business. You are much more than this organization. You are better than this. I know your plan to double cross Raven and Benita. You have no choice. They are planning to kill you. Shanna told me the only reason she was able to save Antonio was that the man was going to shoot you first," Angela stated as a fact.

"Talking about double-crossing, you and Antonio had plans for that for some time. I knew it for a long time. I do my homework. You and Antonio were lovers about 20 years ago. You and Antonio had a baby that you put up for adoption. Antonio never knew about him. I let you two play your little games. I bet you don't know who found out about you and Antonio. I don't care about you and Antonio. When I get the book, I will be powerful enough to rule the world," exclaimed David.

"Who got you that information?" asked Angela. "From someone you would least expect. From someone on the inside," David stated. "I presume your daughter, Mary,"

Angela replied. "Oh no, little girl, it is someone else. They have a saying in this group: Once a scorpion, always a scorpion. I like this game we are playing. In fact, Angela, I have always thought of you as someone that could take over from me. My daughter has some weaknesses that you don't," said David. "Mary seems to be able to take care of herself. I heard that she shot several of the attackers herself. Maybe your little girl has grown up. Antonio said that she was becoming more like you every day. I've be careful about her, if I was you. Let's call a truce about this mess," Angela asked.

David studied Angela for a minute, "I agree. We will sort this out later. We have two enemies we need to take care of first. I want you to stir the pot with Raven and Benita first. Let's see if they can play the game. You are good at that. Now go and be seen around. Make it look like we are upset with each other." Angela turned and walked out of the office. She made sure that she yelled back at David, "After all, I do for you that is how you treat me!" Angela smiled to herself thinking David's secretary will have this gossip all over the building in about 20 minutes.

Benita and Raven were in Paris at the fashion show. Benita was showing her winter collection of clothes. Benita's fashion show was a huge success. Raven commented to Benita that she did have a great fashion sense. Benita was staying with Raven in her intimate apartment close to the river.

Benita's cell phone rang about 3 a.m. She answered the phone call when she recognized the number. It was Victoria, David's secretary. "I got the news you wanted me to call you about. Angela is back from wherever she has been. It appears that David wasn't too happy with her. They had a shouting match that could be heard all over the executive floor. I hope you don't mind me calling so late." Benita replied, "Now call my friend Lopez. Tell him I want him to start working tonight. He should call me about what happens." Victoria put down her cell phone to call Lopez from a secure line in the office. Benita told Raven about the phone call. Raven said, "Good, maybe we can get rid of all three of them. Now come to bed."

David worked all day. It was about midnight when he went home. He parked his black limo in his underground garage. He could sense that something felt different. Something was out of place. His home was located out of town in an isolated area. He didn't like neighbors getting into his business.

David took his black suit coat off before going to the elevator. He turned around quickly. Before him were three large oriental men. They were dressed in black martial arts clothing. "Well, David, we have been waiting for you all night. You must be tired from all the work you did today," their leader said to David. "Not really, I have not gotten my work out in yet. I was going to my gym to work out upstairs. It looks like I will be getting a little tonight before I go upstairs," he replied. "I like that you said a little exercise. It shouldn't take that long for us." the leader laughed. "No, I meant that for me. There are only three of you," David said. "That's where you are wrong. There are six," said a man behind one of David's red sports cars with two other men. David knew that voice. It was from one of his personal bodyguards. He thought he could trust him. He should have known better. Wong was one of the best karate masters in the world. Things were starting to get out of David's control.

Another voice spoke, "Now, boys can't a girl get in on some fun." It was a female voice. Wong knew who that was. It had to be Angela. Wong turned around, behind him were two individuals. He couldn't make out who the man was with her. "Now, Wong, it looks like you had just seen a ghost. You should know this man from your martial art matches. I do believe he broke two of your ribs and arm the last time you met.

For the others here, let me introduce him to you, he is Van Lo Sing from San Francisco. The other men looked at each other. They knew they had a chance with Angela and David, but Van Lo Sing was another thing."

David laughed. His evil laugh echoed around the large underground garage. "You know how this is going to end," David softly said. "Let's get this started. Only the winners will walk out of here alive." David moved to the center of the garage. He still had his black suit coat on his arm with him. Angela and Van Lo Sing joined him there. Two of the men started to pull out guns. A shot could be heard. A bullet landed in front of them. "This is going to be a martial arts fight. We will have none of that," said a female voice from the darkest part of the garage.

The two men dropped their guns on the cement floor. All the men rushed at once toward David, Angela and Van Lo Sing. David didn't waste any time. He threw his coat on the man just in front of him and hit him behind the man's right ear. The man was dead before he hit the cement floor. The next man knocked David down. David rolled around on the floor and jumped up as high as he could. He kicked the man in the chest. The man fell backward. He was stunned. Angela had her hands full with two other men. She kicked one of them in the head knocking him down. The other one was more cautious. They moved away from the others. This was going to take some time. She could tell that he was very skillful.

Van Lo Sing had Wong and one of the other men attack him. Wong made the first move. He jumped and kicked. Van Lo Sing jumped over both of them. As he jumped, he caught the second man by the neck. A quick blow to his throat killed the man in an instant. This gave Wong his chance. Wong struck Van Sing in his back. Van Lo Sing was knocked to the cement floor. Van Lo Sing jumped to his feet. He nodded at Wong for his skill. "Let's finish this," Wong yelled at Van Lo Sing. They both leaped at each other. This time only one came down on his feet. The other crashed to the cement floor in a heap.

David was taking his time with his man. They were matching blow for blow. David was able to throw his man over his shoulder. When the man hit the floor, David finished him off with a kick to his throat. David thought to himself, "I need to get in shape. I must be getting old. This took too long."

This left Angela and her last man in battle. David had to say that Angela's opponent was very skilled. Van Lo Sing and he watched. They seemed to enjoy watching such a skillful fight. Finally, Angela got the best of the man. Before she delivered the last blow to her opponent, she said, "I am going to let you live. Go and leave this country. I can tell you that the person who hired you will kill you. They will not forgive you for being alive and us being alive." The young man nodded in respect to Angela. "I am forever in your debt. If you ever need assistance, I will give my life for you. It is my sacred honor to do so." The young man bowed to everyone present and silently left.

David looked at the dark corner in the garage. "Who is there?" he asked. "I am tired of saving your life," Shanna said as she walked out of the darkness. She was very pale. She started to fall. Angela caught her before she hit the cement floor. "How did you know to be here?" Angela asked. "A friend of mine called me. He said there was a price on my head. I was to be taken out tonight. He said there was another big hit on for tonight. It didn't take me long to figure out who the hit was on because of the price of the hit. You had just gotten back. I put two and two together," replied Shanna.

David asked, "Who sent you, Van Lo Sing?" Van Lo Sing answered, "A friend from your past. She said you would know who. She says you owe her for stealing that Chinese Vase."

David only replied as Van Lo Sing left the garage, "Well, I'll be damn."

Chapter VIII
Heading Back:
Will they make it to Eagle Train Station?

They headed back to Eagle Mountain. It would take them three days to get there. One Feather said he would take us a different route. The fall leaves were turning bright colors of red, yellow and gold. The mountains and hills were rich in the colors from the hardwood trees. They were about a day out from Eagle Mountain when One Feather suggested that they stop for the night by a warm spring. They set up camp. There were several apple trees full of red apples. Nick decided that he wanted to stew the apples for dessert for supper.

After supper, everyone went over to the warm spring to soak in the warm almost hot mineral water. This was one of the few times that they had a rest from their long journey. While they were enjoying the warm mineral water, several conversations started up.

Moses asked Antonio to tell him about himself. Antonio had kept his past pretty- well secret. Everyone was caught off guard when Antonio started to talk. "Well, I don't have much to tell. I don't know my parents. They died right after I was born. My father was Italian, and my mother was a Mayan Priest. My father had joined up with some Spanish explorers to come to America to find treasure and gold. The only thing my father found was my mother. The only thing both found was sickness and death. I was raised by my mother's family. They went deep into the jungles of South America to escape from the fighting of the Spanish and natives. A great Medicine Man taught me many things such as magic and languages. I found that I had the ability to learn almost any language very quickly. One day, I ran away from the jungle. The great Medicine Man had gotten jealous of me. I thought he was going to kill me. I guess, I have been running ever since," answered Antonio.

Moses laughed at Antonio, "You expect us to believe that story. That would make you several centuries old." Antonio replied back, "Yes, that would. It does make a good story doesn't it, John." John laughed and said, "No, some of that story might be true. I heard that Antonio is much older. There's a rumor that Antonio was the last survivor from Atlantis," John said with a smile. That's when everyone laughed. Everyone laughed except Lo Ming. She wondered if it was John or Antonio telling the truth. She decided that a little bit of both stories might be true. She was glad that nobody ever asked her anything about herself. She would have to make up a story like those two.

The fall moon was bright in the sky. The night was cool. Soon everyone went back to their tents. Antonio asked John if Little Wolf could spend the night in his tent. "I want Little Wolf to read some of *The Book of Fall* to me. It might be good to see how much ancient language he knows. If anything were to happen to me, it would be good to have another interpreter." Antonio did make sense. John nodded his head in agreement. Antonio was right. This could be very advantageous. The Red Woman had told John that Little Wolf had talents in memorizing everything by making a picture of it in his mind.

Mary asked John what Antonio was doing with Little Wolf. John told her about Antonio teaching Little Wolf about *The Book of Fall*. Mary told John she wasn't so sure that was a good idea. She was worried about Little Wolf's safety.

The next day the group went by an area of the land called **The Breadbasket** of **The Land of the Eagle Feathers.** There were fields of wheat, oats, corn and squash. There were several fields of vegetables and orchards of fruit trees. It would soon be time to harvest everything. They had a special festival for this called **The Gathering.** Even though, they were in a hurry to get back, they had to stay a few days to help with the harvest. John didn't like the delay. He knew better than to go on to the Eagle Train Station.

I got the group together. I told them that we must take a couple of days to assist with the harvest. Two days wouldn't make too much of a difference. I needed the time to check on a few things. Mary liked the idea of having two more days to be around Little Wolf. Little Wolf and Mary had become closer. They were spending time together. Mary was teaching Little Wolf how to become a better archer with his bow and arrow. We watched her making bullseyes at various distances. It wasn't long before Little Wolf hit those targets with as much skill as Mary. I didn't say anything because I knew that Little Wolf was already a good archer. He did improve some.

The next two days everyone pitched in to help with the harvest. Lo Ming and Moses went to the river to harvest wild rice. Lo Ming was very skillful with the canoe. Moses wasn't so much. He almost capsized their canoe. Antonio, Nick and Rose worked in the grain fields cutting down the grain stalks. June, One Feather and Mary removed the grains from the stalks by having horses walk over the grain shafts. I thought this was good to get everyone's mind off of what was going to happen when we get back. We would be lucky to survive with everyone after us.

I went over to the Great Elder to talk to him. He was in his Long House. He beckoned for me to come in to talk to him. I sat down cross-legged in front of him. "What can I do for you,

John?" he asked. "I have not seen Red Woman. I need to talk to her," I answered. "She is gone. I am not sure where she went. I fear she has gone to that place on the other side called Houston. I think she wants to see the one that once was her husband, David," the Great Elder replied. "I was afraid of that. This whole quest for the books has some serious consequences. Mary does not know what to do. Little Wolf is wondering who his father is. Angela and my friend, Shanna, may be in serious trouble," I stated to him.

"I wouldn't worry too much about them. I think they can take care of themselves. I worry more about you and your group. You have many enemies that will try to either take *The Book of Fall* away from you or kill you before you can get back by the first day of Winter. John, you are in a bad situation. I don't have to tell you that there will be many people waiting for you on the other side of the tunnel. I don't see how you can survive to get through them," warned the Great Elder.

"You are wise, Great Elder. I have been trying to think of another way to get out of here. We need to get *The Book of Fall* to the Museum in Houston to decipher it. It has the final clues for the location for *The Book of Winter* hidden in it," I told the Great Elder.

"White Elk is your answer to that problem. If there is another way to get across or though the mountain range to get you back, he would know. He may not want to show you. To use the mystic passage that is rumored to exist will weaken the barrier that keeps the outsiders out. Judging from the strength of the barriers we have in place; it will be too weak to keep any outsider out by the first day of Winter.

Outsiders will flood our land and destroy us and our precious resources when the barriers fail. The last time that happened many people died, including you. We cannot have that type of blood bath happen again. If you have anyone die on either side, you will be held accountable. You will be banished from **The Land of the Eagle Feathers** forever. Leaders are held accountable in this land. Spend some time with your son. I have seen your destiny in the smoke of my lodge. You have precious little time left here. You have been a great warrior for many circles of the sun. I have always treated you as a son. I will miss you, John. Only the Great Spirits know your destiny. Little Wolf is my great-grandson. I will take care of him, if you cannot," the Great Elder said with sadness.

I looked at the Great Elder. "I have known for some time that I have only a slight chance to live. My only chance is to find *The Book of Winter*. Without its powers, I will die on the first day of the new year. I don't regret my life. I have lived many years. I have fought many great battles in many faraway lands. I will do my best to save this land. Failure is not an option. I have a son and many friends that depend on me. My destiny is written in the stars. Please send for White Elk! I will need to talk to him after the harvest ceremony tonight. I will meet with him by the Great White Oak tree." I nodded my head to show respect to the Great Elder as I left the Long House. He nodded back. I saw something that I had never seen before. The Great Elder had a tear in his right eye.

Everyone worked until it was getting dark. The harvest had been a good one. Corn and other grains were stored in clay pots in several rooms of a nearby cave. The apples and other fruit were picked. Some of the fruit were left to dry in the fall sun. The cool caves that dotted the Eagle Mountain allowed for natural storage. The constant temperature of the caves preserved the food.

Several of the older women had cooked all day for the harvest festival called **The Gathering** in **The Land of the Eagle Feathers**. They had made a sweet corn soup to be shared during the ceremony to celebrate a good harvest.

June remembered a legend about how the Cherokee learned to plant corn or maize. There once was the first woman called Selu. She was the goddess of maize which we now call corn. Her two sons thought Selu had gotten too powerful. They were afraid of her. They tried to kill her. Before she died, she taught both of her sons that her dying wish was to show them how to plant and farm maize. This was to give her people a food source forever. Her sons followed her instructions and taught the tribe how to farm corn. Because she did this, her spirit is resurrected with each harvest.

June noticed that The Gathering Festival was a mixture of several different harvest festivals she had studied. For example, the sweet corn soup was an Iroquois tradition. The Cherokee celebrated the harvest at the first October new moon which would be tonight. The Cherokee believed that the world was created during the autumn of the year. Several other tribes would celebrate corn which was the main stay of food during the winter months. The Creek, Seminole, Yuchi, Iroquois and Cherokee called this festival The Green Corn Festival. This festival was tradition held any time after the corn became ripe enough to eat.

The one thing that all these traditions had was to thank the great spirits for a good harvest. There would be dancing, singing, rituals and prayer. June told everyone to put on any bright clothing they had and join in the celebration. We were to be guests of honor. Everyone felt that we, **The Keepers of the Yawi,** had brought them a good harvest.

As soon as everyone got dressed in their finest clothing, the Great Elder had everyone sit in a semi-circle. He raised his hands and recited an ancient prayer to the great spirits of the land. He thanked them for a good harvest. He took out a long wooden pipe that was decorated with pictures of corn and other grains with feathers attached to it with leather strings. He lit the pipe that was filled with some type of herb. He held the pipe high and took several puffs of smoke into his lungs. He looked at the moon and let out a large puff of smoke toward it. He then took one long puff and pointed the pipe toward each direction letting out a puff in that direction until he had the directions of North, East, South and West covered.

In the background, drums and singing could be heard. That was the signal to begin the dancing and other events of the night. The dancing and singing would last until late in the night. There was plenty of food and drink for everyone. June made sure that each one of our group took part.

The women danced with the women dancers, and the men danced with the men dancers. Each danced in circles around one another. It surprised nobody that Antonio was a great dancer. Moses danced in his own version of dancing and singing from the Outback. He enchanted everyone with his playing of the Didgeridoo that he had brought along.

I left the festival at the height of the celebration. I had a meeting to attend with White Elk. It was only a few minutes' walk to the Great White Oak Tree near the ridgeline of the mountaintop. The bright new moon lit the path. I saw White Elk in his white elk robe standing under the tree. The mountain air here was a little cool. White Elk did not turn around as I approached him. I stopped about 10 feet from him.

Without turning around White Elk spoke, "I see you found the book. I was worried that you would not make it back. The Harpies were more than you could have handled." "I was glad you helped us," I replied. "Now, you come to me for some more assistance. You want to get out of this land without being noticed by those that want to stop you," he said to me. "Yes, we need some more of your generous help. I know that you know a way out of this land that would bypass the tunnel. If we go through the tunnel, there will be much blood shed. I cannot lose anyone. I have to have all my group to obtain *The Book of Winter*," I reminded him.

"Yes, I know. Whenever we can avoid needless killing, we should try to avoid it. I do know another passage to get out of **The Land of the Eagle Feathers** without being seen. However, it is dangerous and could have severe consequences for this land. It will weaken the ability to keep the outsiders out." I interrupted White Elk by saying, "Does it matter? The barriers are weak now. It will only be a matter of a few more weeks before they are able to breech the barriers anyway." "Why do you think I am here to help you? I will help you under one condition. You must settle this once and for all. If it means that you must kill and be banished from this land, you must promise me that you will. I am tired of all this fighting and want **The Land of the Eagle Feathers** to survive. Your destiny is going to be a difficult one for you to follow. The sands of time are catching up with you. They are catching up with me. Your son and future are at stake. We will leave at noon tomorrow. Have your group meet me here by this tree and bring Little Wolf with you. We will need him to help get the passage open. He has great powers. He is much like you, John." Before I could say anything, White Elk faded into the darkness.

Moses and Lo Ming had left the festival just before it ended. They wanted to spend some time together alone from the others. They found a grassy spot about two hundred yards from the festival. They sat down together and laid in the dry autumn grass. Moses took Lo Ming into his arms. It was so nice and peaceful here. They could hear the singing and drum music in the distance. Moses loved looking at Lo Ming in the moonlight. Her long shiny black hair highlighted her beautiful oriental face. They watched the bright night sky. There were several shooting stars that lit up the sky. Moses gave Lo Ming a passionate kiss. He told her that in the Outback in Australia that was a sign of true love. Lo Ming told him that sounds good, but he just probably made that up. Moses said back that in **The Land of the Eagle Feathers** you can't make anything up. If you believe hard enough, it will come true. "Well Moses, then I will take your word for it. I have always believed in you," Lo Ming said as she kissed him back.

Antonio, Nick and Rose decided to call it a night. There was a couple of rooms in the main Long House that they had been told to use. They started talking about what they would find when they got back. "You do know that there will be many people wanting to either kill us or take the book or both," Antonio told them. "I was thinking about that. We would be crazy to leave this land the same way we came in. Everyone and their brother will be waiting for us," said Nick.

Rose said that she had overheard John and the Great Elder talk about another way out of here that bypasses the tunnel. There was something about White Elk knowing a passage." "I hope you are right, Rose. Our lives will depend on that. I do know one thing. We will all have to stay close together to survive. When we get to Houston, I will grab the notes and books I need, and we must leave the city before anyone knows we have been there," said Antonio.

"Where will we go until you get the book deciphered to find *The Book of Winter*? Nick asked. "I know of a place in the swamps of Louisiana that nobody ever goes?" said Rose. "How do you know of such a place?" asked Antonio. "It's where my parents live. If I hadn't been born there, even I would not go there. Don't worry, they have their own way of powering lights and electrical equipment. However, they do have spiders and snakes, but don't worry about that either. They were my play friends when I was a child," said Rose with a laugh.

Mary had been dancing with Little Wolf. They were having a fun time together. Mary was starting to get tired. Little Wolf suggested that they go and sit by some boulders away from the festival. Mary took Little Wolf's hand, and they walked over to the boulders. As they started to be seated, Mary slipped falling to the ground. Her head hit one of the boulders. She saw a big flash. As she started to get up, Little Wolf told her to lie down and not move. He had to be sure that she was not hurt. Mary did as she was told.

Mary told Little Wolf to get Rose. She did not feel well. Her head felt like it was spinning like a top. "I will lie here until you come back with Rose." After Little Wolf left, Mary passed out. She had several dreams. One dream was very real. It was her father pointing a gun at a man. The man was telling David, her father, that she was not to see that man again. She remembered saying, "But I love him, I am going to have his child." Her father's face became angrier. He started to pull the gun's trigger. The man grabbed the gun, and there was a fight. During the fight, she felt something hit her in the forehead. Then everything went black.

Mary felt someone shaking her. When she was able to see, it was June. June had some water with some herbs in it. "Drink this, it will help you." June said. Mary did as she was told. Her headache went away. "Don't get up until I say so.
This is a very powerful medicine. It will take a few minutes to work."

Mary could see that Little Wolf was very upset. She told him not to worry. She would be alright in a few minutes. June would be taking good care of her. "Little Wolf go back to the festival and beat your drum and dance. I will be along shortly. I need to talk to June. Now, go and have some fun with those girls that were making eyes at you," ordered Mary. "Then Little Wolf said something that almost knocked Mary down.

Before Little Wolf realized it, he said, "Yes, mother." Little Wolf ran back to the festival. He knew he had said too much.

June looked at Mary's face. "You knew all the time. Didn't you?" asked Mary. "I am a medicine woman. I can see many things that other people don't," June answered back. "You will remember some things. The medicine I gave you will help your memory. Tell me what you saw," demanded June. Mary told her the dream she had. "Who was the man your father was fighting with? What did he look like?" asked June. Mary concentrated as hard as she could. A face started to form in her mind. She heard a voice behind her. She turned her head and saw the man in her dream. "Mary, are you seriously hurt?" John said with a very worried face.

"I will take care of Mary. June, you need to go and be with One Feather. We will be leaving at noon tomorrow. Have Little Wolf come back here to be with us," I stated. "You don't need to do that, John. June can help me to my room in the Long House. You tell Little Wolf that I am alright and that I am going to go to bed. All I need is some rest," Mary said. I did as Mary asked. June helped Mary back to her room and put her to bed. One Feather was waiting on June to be together for the rest of the night. It would be a long night for Mary because her dreams came back.

When she woke in the morning, things were starting to clear up in her mind. She was confused about things. She was very upset. All these years, she did not know. The more she thought about it, the more upset she got. She hated them for it. Why didn't they tell her? She knew better than lose it. She would play along and pretend she didn't know. She would get her revenge on both of them. She wasn't that young woman that John knew long ago. She had a cold side. She must have gotten that from her father.

117

Angela took Shanna up to one of the bedrooms on the third floor on David's mansion. They used the service elevator. Shanna was able to walk with Angela's help. Angela put Shanna on the bedroom's queen size bed. She told Shanna to get some sleep. She would go to the hospital and tell Nick's parents where Shanna was. Shanna was worried that someone might go after Nick's parents. "Don't worry, I have a man that is good at hiding them until we can find a safe space for everyone. Get some sleep, we have a big day ahead of us tomorrow. By the way, I put your gun on the night table next to the bed. One thing I do know, David will always protect you. He may have an evil streak. He may be a dishonest man. There is one thing about him. He is never ungrateful. He will pay you back handsomely," whispered Angela.

"Yes, I know. David and I have a deal. No matter whatever happens to me, he will protect Nick and his parents. He knows I have enemies from business dealings I have done in the past. He told me that there is a price on my head for not killing Nick. He said that he knows who those people are. David wouldn't tell me who they were. He made me promise not to kill them if I found out. He wanted to do that himself," Shanna said before she drifted off to sleep.

Angela heard a noise behind her. It was David and his personal bodyguard, Wong. "I thought Van Lo Sing killed you," Angela said in a surprised voice. "No, I am sorry to say that I faked my death. Van Lo Sing would have killed me. He is better than me. I have the utmost respect for him. That is why I went down so easily," said Wong.

David looked at Angela, "I have known for some time that Raven and Benita were going to try something like this. How better than have my personal bodyguard become part of the plot to kill me! Raven and Benita have been planning to get rid of me for years. Let me tell you a little secret. When I saw the

Red Woman alive, I started to think about things. It took time for me to put the pieces together. I ran that moment over and over in my mind. You were not surprised to see her. It took more time to find out the answer. I found out that Raven and Benita had taken a contract out to kill my wife. Rumors are that you and several others took that contract. It seems that you were the only one that survived to get paid. That was about twenty years ago. It was about the time that you were in the hospital for several serious wounds. You saved my wife, didn't you?"

A voice behind them spoke, "The answer is yes. She did. It almost cost her everything." David and Wong turned around. David could not believe it. His former wife, the Red Woman, was standing there at the bedroom's door. David's face was pale. It was like he had seen someone come back from the dead. In the Red Woman's hand was a pearl handled revolver that David had given her many years ago.

Angela sarcastically said, "Well, I will see you two lovebirds later. Wong nodded at Angela in agreement. David said to Wong, "You know what to do. Wong said, "Yes, sir. I will see you tomorrow night about 12 p.m. at the underground safe." Both Angela and Wong left the bedroom together. They were glad to be leaving. Wong only hoped that David's former wife, Donna, didn't kill him. David had told him he would pay him handsomely for his help. He didn't worry about David double crossing him. He had saved David's life numerous times. David had a thing about that. Wong smiled to himself. This was the only reason he was still alive. Most of David's close employees were either dead from him or dead from his enemies.

Angela was in a hurry. She had to get to the motel where she had hidden Nick's parents. Things were starting to unravel here. There were rumors on the street about a hostile takeover of David's company. "Hostile takeover is an understatement," she thought. Angela wondered who would be the one that would kill Raven and Benita. Would it be David or the Red Woman? They should be the ones that should be given the first crack at them.

Wong called Raven. The conversation was short. "David is dead. I lost my best men in the process. Put the money in my offshore account. I have his bloody suit to prove it. I will leave it in his office. I will see you when you get back in two days." He hung up the phone. Wong knew Raven wouldn't send people to kill him. She was one that didn't leave any witness around. She was one that usually did her own dirty work. She liked to see people die. He would be safe until Raven got back. He had to tell the members of the board that David was dead and give them some details of what had happened to him.

"What are we going to do now, Donna, or should I call you Red Woman? David said. "We are going to go to your den and talk. I will do most of the talking. I could kill you, and nobody would ever know I did it. You see, everyone thinks I'm dead. She put the gun in her suit pocket. Do you like my clothes? Angela said they are very fashionable when she gave them to me two days ago," she smiled. "Yes, they are. Angela always had good taste in clothes. Like her, they fit you in all the right places," David smiled as he led the way to his den. David's heart was beating wildly in his chest. He didn't care if she killed him. He deserved it. If he was going to die, he would rather it to be her instead of some cowardly stranger.

Down the hall was his den. He unlocked the door. He motioned for Donna to go in first. Donna shook her head. She knew better. David went in and turned on the light. He asked to be seated behind his desk. Donna nodded yes. He sat down in a thick black leather chair. Donna took a seat in a comfortable chair in front of the desk. She took out her gun and pointed at him. A reflection on a painting got her eye. She turned her head and saw something she could not believe. On the front wall of the den was a full-length painting of her. She looked at David. "I never let anyone in this den. It has special locks on the door and alarms. You are the only one that has ever seen that picture," David softly said as he looked into her eyes.

She did not want to believe anything that David would tell her. "It has been a long time since I have been in this house. You have not changed anything. Why is that?" she asked. "You should know the answer to that question," replied David. "Do not give me that you are still in love with me crap, David. I know better," Donna sarcastically answered back.

"I am curious. Why did you come back here? You could have stayed in **The Land of the Eagle Feathers** and been relatively safe," asked David. "You know me, I don't like to leave unfinished business. David, you are unfinished business. We were once very much in love many years ago. I had left **The Land of the Eagle Feathers** to spy on you. The Great Elder needed to know more about you. He thought that if someone could get your trust, he could get information that could help him stop you. My problem was that I got too close to you. I fell in love with you. When Mary came along, I had to stay. I thought having a child would somehow change you, but I was wrong. It didn't change you one bit." Donna said with a hint of hate.

"David replied, "When I discovered that you were from The Land of the Eagle Feathers, I felt betrayed. I thought our marriage was a sham. I started to hate you. The more I tried to hate you the more I figured out that I loved you. I was too deep into **The Omen** to get out. I do admit that I loved the power too much. I was a greedy, power hungry young man then. I really thought about getting out. The only way I could have done that was to gain control of **The Omen**. I would have to become the Chairman of the Board of Directors. The only way to do that was to conquer **The Land of the Eagle Feathers**. If I had done that, I would have had total control. I would have been too powerful for anyone to stop me. You see, I was in a catch 22. If I conquered **The Land of the Eagle Feathers,** you would have left me or killed me. If I didn't conquer **The Land of the Eagle Feathers, The Omen** would kill me for being a failure. When I thought you were dead due to a car wreck, I lost it. I became my old evil self. You must admit that I almost conquered **The Land of the Eagle Feathers** the last time I tried," David laughed.

Donna had been listening to David carefully. "I don't have much to say about that. You see, Raven and Mary had asked me to attend an important meeting. They said it involved you getting a promotion to Chairman of the Board. Naturally I went to the meeting. It was to be held at the old mansion in the Redwood Estates. They said it had to be a secret meeting because they didn't want you to get advanced notice. They wanted to throw a big conference meeting and program to surprise you. I saw it as a chance to change things. I should have known. It was a trap. Angela and several other men were there instead. Raven and Benita were not. For some reason, Angela killed the other men and saved me. Later, she told me it was for redemption for leaving **The Land of the Eagle Feathers** without her Grandfather's permission.

I got badly hurt in the fight. She did too. She took some of my jewelry and clothing and put it in my car. One of her crew was a woman about the same height and build as me. She drove my car with the dead woman in it and jumped out as it went over the cliff by White Canyon. The car burst into flames and nobody ever questioned that the woman in it wasn't me. Angela hid me until we got better. When I got better, she took me to the entrance **to The Land of the Eagle Feathers** and left me. You can guess the rest of the story," Donna told David.

"That's a nice story. You did leave a few things out. Like when you took Mary's child from the hospital after her son was born. To hide the fact, he had been kidnapped. I thought it was best to make up the dying at childbirth story. That would have been the best for Mary. Mary had been in a coma and I didn't have to explain anything to Mary for almost nine months until she came out of the coma," David said without any regrets.

Donna took out her gun and pointed it at David. "Judging by what I have seen tonight, you are in serious trouble. Raven and Benita are planning to take over. David, you are on your way out. Don't worry, I won't kill you. I need you to take care of those two. Do you have the nerve to kill your second wife? You didn't have the nerve to kill me." Donna smiled at him.

"Even if I did kill them, I would still have to go after **The Land of the Eagle Feathers.** I need the power of *The Book of Winter* to survive. Having the book would change everything. I would be too powerful for anyone to mess with me!" declared David. "Well. I see you have not changed David. That's why I am here. I will need to stop you somehow?" Donna replied. Donna aimed her gun and fired five rounds in David's direction.

John had everyone ready to go at noon. White Elk was in the lead. John followed him. John had told everyone about trying a different way out of **The Land of the Eagle Feathers**. Everyone agreed that to go the usual way could be disaster. There could be several different groups waiting for them to exit the land.

Antonio couldn't wait to see Angela. He missed her. He was worried that David's enemies would want her out of the way. Nick was going out of his mind. He was very upset about

Shanna. He had been away too long. There were many things that could go wrong while he was gone.

Rose was another matter. She was wondering where Zan could be in this vast land. She hoped that somehow, she could find him. She had asked several different chiefs and Spiritual Leaders, but nobody seemed to know anything. There was only one other that could know. White Elk seemed to know everything about this land. She would ask him when she got the chance.

They had traveled for about five hours. White Elk signaled for them to make camp by a mountain stream. It didn't take long for the camp to be set up. They were a well-oiled machine by now. Nick had the fire going. He was cooking a meat like dish. The natives here called it "fake meat stew." They had given him some type of wheat and oak protein that first needed boiled. Then it was to be shaped into patties like hamburger and cooked in an iron pan. He put onions in the iron pan with several herbs and other spices he had found. He used some vegetable oil in a small container to fry the patties. He added some potatoes he had been given for helping with the harvest.

The smell from the cooking floated around the camp. Moses always felt that food cooked outside smelled better than food cooked indoors. It wasn't long before the meal was done. Nick and Rose dished out the food to everyone. Antonio was surprised that the patties tasted like chicken. Mary thought they tasted like fish. Moses thought they tasted like beef. June laughed.

When June was asked why she laughed, she answered. "I have heard of such a dish. Legends say that an ancient tribe once thought that killing animals for food was barbaric. They worked on a substitute for animal meat. After many long years, they found a special plant that could be added to wheat and oatmeal that would turn it into a meat like dish. The strange thing about it was that when fried into patties it would taste different to different people. It seemed to have a quality to make people think about their favorite meat. This in turn made the patties taste different to each person. If you liked chicken, it would taste like chicken. If you liked lamb, beef or pork, it would taste like that meat. Now you know why people here do not hunt animals. They don't need to. They have this to replace it. Don't get any ideas on taking this to the outside world. It doesn't work there very well. However, I think that scientists are getting closer to finding a replacement there."

After their evening meal, Rose asked White Elk if they could have a private talk. White Elk said he would be glad to talk to her. He wanted to ask her some questions in return. He said that they could talk after everyone had gone to bed for the night. He would sit up by the campfire. She said that she would be there. It was about 10 o'clock when everyone finally settled down to sleep. Rose waited 30 minutes before she got up to approach White Elk.

White Elk motioned for Rose to sit down on a log beside him. The evening stars covered the sky. The moon was just a sliver in the southeastern sky. "What is troubling you, Rose?' he asked. "I have a close friend that I need to know of his whereabouts in **The Land of the Eagle Feathers**. He apparently was sent somewhere in these lands," she answered him.

White Elk took both of Rose's hands in his. He concentrated for a few seconds. "Child, he is more than a friend. He was once supposed to marry you. I know of the wizard that is his father. Zorn is a man that is not of the best disposition. He likes to take revenge on anyone that he feels has gone against his wishes. I do not know where he sent his son. I do have some idea. Zan is where I cannot feel him. There is only one place where that can be. It is a land that people here call: The

Land of Nightmares. The problem is nobody here knows where it is.

Some say it is in a different dimension. Many great thinkers have thought that there are several dimensions stacked on top of each other. They believe that the only way to get to these dimensions were through Black Holes in space. At least, that's what people in the world on the other side of the tunnel think. I don't believe in that stuff. I believe there must be an easier way to get to them. I know you have traveled to other dimensions. The Land of Nightmares exists between consciousness and subconsciousness. The Great Elder and other medicine people believe that is where the Great Medicine man might have taken *The Book of Winter*.

I believe that *The Book of Fall* will lead you to a portal to The Land of Nightmares. If your lover is there, I only hope he is still sane. The Land of Nightmares is just that. It is a land where you must confront your worst Nightmare. The only way out once you go in is to defeat your own worst Nightmare. Very few have ever come out alive from that land. Zorn must have been sent there for evil deeds he had done. He must have defeated his Nightmare. That is the only way he could have been able to send Zan there. I will not tell anyone about our conversation. Your only hope is that everyone goes into the portal to The Land of Nightmares together.

You will need to take Little Wolf and three others with your group. The Red Woman, One Feather and the evil one called David. Only evil can defeat evil. Once your group gets into the land, Zorn will come to destroy you, Rose. David is the only one evil enough to do that. Do not trust David. David has a past that only I know. Only the Red Woman and his daughter can defeat him. I hope I am wrong about this. If I am right, there is a good chance that you and your group will never come back from that land. At least, you might have Zan to spend eternity with. Do not tell anyone about our conversation. They must go into the land because they are willing to go. You will have to have a conversation with all of them if that is where you are going. Again, let me be clear: they all must go willingly. I trust they will make the right decision. I know David will go. He was always the one that wanted it all for himself. He is too much like his father.

Before Rose could ask White Elk any more questions, White Elk left her. Rose decided she had learned enough from White Elk. She would use the knowledge that White Elk had given her. She would do everything in her power to guide their group to come back and find the portal to The Land of Nightmares. Her longing for Zan was almost too much for her to endure. She was so close to finding her love. Yet, he was so far away. Rose knew that she must kept control of her emotions. She had too much at stake for the others to think that she was only on this quest for selfish reasons. She would convince them to take David with them even if they didn't want to take him.

One Feather and June were madly in love. They would spend every night together. They knew that they had only one night left before June and the others would be going back to the Eagle Train Station. Snow and Midnight were running wild in the forest. When wolves mate, they mate for life. June told One Feather she was going to let Midnight stay with Snow until she got back from the outside world. One Feather told her that she could not do that. Midnight could help her on the other side. She might need Midnight's help to keep her safe. Reluctantly, June agreed with One Feather.

June and One Feather enjoyed being outside. Each night, they put their blankets each together outside the camp. As they talked and cuddled together, they talked about their future. One Feather told her that he had a feeling that Angela and Antonio were more than what they told others. He felt a closeness to them. June looked at One Feather, "If what I think is true, I will become close to them also. We will have to wait for answers. Destiny has a way of going full circle. There is one thing that I know. Both Angela and Antonio speak many dialects of Native Indian languages. I have heard them talking to each other. They are in love much like we are." The next morning, One Feather and June woke up to find Midnight and Snow beside them. Snow had his head on top of Midnight's back. "They do make a lovely couple," June said.

The group got up and started toward the southeast. White Elk told them it would take them about a whole day to get to where they were going. Even though he was much older than anyone there, he kept up a fast pace. They were in pasture country with rolling hills and high grass. The grass was starting to die from the lack of rain and the shorter days. They saw a lot of elk, deer and buffalo. Winter would be hard on these large animals. They were trying to build up fat supplies for the long winter by eating as much grass as they could. Nick noted that the animals didn't appear to be afraid of them. This he thought was because nobody hunted them.

It was late afternoon when White Elk told them to pitch camp. There was a small river near to get water and some fish for supper. Nick spotted some wild onions and other vegetables to eat. Moses noted that the river went straight into the side of a mountain. It didn't take anyone long to figure that the way out had to be using the river passage into the mountain. The only problem would be without an air tank, you would have to hold your breath until you got to the other side of the mountain. This could be a problem if you got caught on any obstacle under the water. This would be a hazardous way out.

I told everyone to pitch their tents. It looked like we might get a heavy rain tonight. The thought of heavy rain and diving in the mountain river did not appear to be a good idea. Nick fixed a good supper. He found some wild pumpkins and made a pudding out of it for dessert. Nobody did much talking.

When the meal was finished, I told everyone what they had already guessed. "We will have to dive under the mountain to get out of **The Land of the Eagle Feathers.** Now I know what you are thinking. The rain will only make the passage more dangerous under the mountain. That is not true. The pressure of the water rushing under the mountain will help us. We will not have to hold our breaths as long. It will push us through the passage faster. The real danger is for the first one that goes through. They must go through and stop in midair on the other side of the mountain. There is a large waterfall at the other end that goes down several hundred feet. The person then must swing themselves over to one side of the waterfall."

"Then what?" asked Rose. "They will tie a knot at the end of the rope to mark where the people holding the rope for others will need to stop the line when other people go through to keep them from falling down the waterfalls on the other side. The first one through will have to tug on the rope sharply three times for us to stop their descent before they go too far down the waterfall. After they have arrived safety, they will tug three times, and we will pull the line back to us for the next one to go down. The last one to go will have One Feather, Little Wolf and White Elk to stop them. That means the last one of us will need to be the lightest person. It will take a lot of strength for three people to hold them. After the last one gets through the underwater passage, they will tie the rope to our packs and send them down."

"Well John, you make it sound so easy. If for any reason the rope breaks, that person will not survive the fall down the waterfall. I know you have brought a lot of rope. But that rope will have to take a lot of stress to do what you are saying. This is risky at best. The one person that has to make it is Antonio

129

and the book," said Moses. "I guess that I will have to go first because I am the heaviest person here. That should be fun. I know you probably think that from the Outback of Australia, I probably wouldn't be a strong swimmer. You don't know that I once wrestled a crocodile on a bet for a hundred pounds of silver. What made it hard was that it was flood season, and I had to do it in the river."

"Well, did you win?" asked Nick. "These boots are made of crocodile skins. I had to teach him a lesson. He had tried to eat a couple of kids the day before. He would have killed someone if I didn't kill him. The reason I wrestled him was to make sure I got the right one. He had a scar on his stomach. See the slight scar on my left boot." said Moses pointing to his left boot.

"That settles who will go first. Now who should go last?" I asked. Lo Ming spoke up first, "I will go last. I am strong and thin. You will need to have someone that has a gymnastic background to swing themselves quickly to one side without jarring the rope out of the holders' hands." "Then it is settled. Please pack only the minimal number of items in your packs. I suggest you pack only your weapons and one dry suit of clothes and a towel. We can come back later when we finish getting *The Book of Winter* to get them," I told them. The only one that said anything was Antonio, "Now that is the most optimistic thing, I have ever heard John say." They couldn't help but laugh. I didn't know if they thought it was funny or that they laughed out of nerves.

Before the group broke up for the night, White Elk wanted to talk to them. "I know that you are getting close to the end of your quest for *The Book of Winter*. There will be many thoughts entering your minds. Some of those thoughts will be that if you could get control of the book, you could become the most powerful person in the Universe. Why should anyone have control of the book besides me? You might rationalize that by getting control of the book, you could save this land besides making yourself rich and powerful. Every one of your group have different reasons for being here. Not all of you are what others know you to be. Remember, to obtain the book, you must work together. Some of you have destinies that lie far beyond this land. We will see if every one of you, follows your destiny. I hope you do. For some of you, I have my doubts. I will see you in the morning at first light. Have a good night's sleep!"

Moses and Lo Ming went back to their tent. They had put their tents together to make a larger one. Moses talked to Lo Ming's mind. He asked her if she was worried about tomorrow. Lo Ming reminded him that she was a warrior, and warriors don't get scared. Moses took Lo Ming into his arms. He kissed her passionately. She responded to his caresses. They made love being very mindful of each other. They took their time. They wanted it to last as long as possible.

Later that night, Moses couldn't help it. He still thought that Lo Ming wasn't telling him everything. He had always wondered why Lo Ming had volunteered to come on this journey. Most people here had reasons connected to this land or someone connected to the land. As far as he knew, she did not. He brushed these thoughts aside and fell asleep in Lo Ming's arms.

I asked White Elk to talk to me. We went off some distance from the campsite near the river to talk. The sounds of the strong flowing river would make it hard for anyone to listen to our conversation. "Is this where Angela was able to get out of The Land of the Eagle Feathers?" I asked White Elk. "John, how did you know that?" White Elk asked. 'I found her over twenty years ago by a deep pool of water about fifty feet down from a large waterfall that came out of one of the mountains on the other side of this land. The pool of water was deep enough to break her fall without hurting her too badly. She was dazed but alright."

"So, you were the one that saved her," White Elk exclaimed. "Yes, I was. I was looking for any cracks or breaks in the mountains that might let anyone break into this land. I took her back with me to the Eagle Mountain Train Station. She never said much about how she came to be in that pool of water. I guessed that she had escaped, as she would have called it, from **The Land of the Eagle Feathers**. Her clothing gave her away that she had to be from this land. She was wearing an Indian dress with symbols of White Elks running," I replied back to him.

"Angela was a problem child. Her mother had a time trying to raise her. She rebelled against anything or anyone. She had told my wife that she wanted to go and find the Red Woman. I told her that the Great Elder would not let her do any such thing. If she left this land without permission, the Great Elder would never let her back in to this land. As you know, she did it anyway. The Great Elder was worried that she might cause problems for the Red Woman if she found her. I guess, we were all wrong about that!" What did you do with her? asked White Elk.

I told White Elk the whole story. I took Angela to the Eagle Train Station. Angela was a young girl about 17 years of age. She was very smart. She was a natural athlete. She wanted me to train her in the martial arts and with weapons. I resisted at first, she had a way of getting you to do things you necessarily wouldn't. After about a year of training, I told her that she must learn to be a woman of culture to fit in to the modern world. The old man at the Eagle Train Station said he had a sister that could do just that. Her name was Grandy. She had an old bed and breakfast in a town not too far away. I gave her to the Old Man and his dog to take her there. When I came back a year later, Grandy said she had taken off and went to Houston, Texas. Grandy said she had never seen anything like her. Angela would read anything she could get her hands on. She learned manners and social graces. Grandy did say one thing: Angela had an obsession about a woman called the Red Woman. Just before she left, she said that she had found her."

"That's a good story, but why are you telling me this now, John?" White Elk asked. "First, if Angela did use this passage to get outside this land, it would make it much easier for us to get out of here. Second, I thought I would need to tell you. You knew that all along, didn't you? I asked White Elk. White Elk nodded his head.

White Elk asked, "What was the reason that Angela turned on you? I understand that she tried several times to kill you." "Well, that is between Angela and me. It had to do with some things I did years later. It is better to ask her. I think she will change her mind about that sometime," I replied. "Oh, you mean when you killed her lover, many years ago. How did you know that? I asked. "I follow your destiny in the stars at night and in the grains of the future sands. She never believed that her lover was going to kill her. You did what was right. Lovers never see very far. I thank you for that. That is why I taught you the mystical arts. I owed you that much. You saved my daughter's life. To which, I will always be grateful," White Elk smiled back. "It was my destiny to save her. She saved the Red Woman. It's funny how things seem to go in circles," I said with great respect

White Elk added one more thing: "It's ironic. The Great Elder forgave Angela a long time ago. Angela saved his daughter, the Red Woman. It almost cost Angela her life. He realized it was her destiny. He is just too proud to tell her so."

It rained after midnight. A thunderstorm came in from the west. The ground became muddy, and the grass was slick. Footing on the steep sides of the river below them made it difficult to climb down to the water below. Moses didn't like the look of the river. It was muddy and swift. He was worried that the lack of visibility in the water would make going through the underground passage too dangerous. It was one thing doing this when the water was clear. He felt it was just too dangerous for anyone to attempt diving and letting the current take them to the other end of the passage in these conditions.

"You are right to think that way Moses. It is too dangerous to do what you have planned. There is another way to do this. We could block the tunnel for the few minutes, and everyone could run down to the other end. The only problem with that is that any dam that we would put up to stop the river flow would flood the whole valley," suggested White Elk.

Antonio spoke up, "Last night, I took a walk up the river valley. There is another branch of this river that forks to the south. We don't have to flood the whole valley if we did this right. We could dam this fork of the river and divert the water to the south fork of the river. The south branch of this river looks like it hasn't had enough water to flow for many years. A dam about 30 feet high would be all we would need to rise the water high enough to start the river flowing down the south branch. It is a waste of good water for the water to keep going out of this land instead of keeping it for use here."

"How do you know this will work?" asked Rose. "I did the same thing many years ago for a general that needed to get his elephants across a deep mountain river in the Alps. It worked very well except I did flood the Po Valley a little. I was a good engineer in my time. We have all the materials we need to do this. Rose, do you still have some of your exploding beads? I will need them. You see those two large boulders on the steep side of the river to the north of us," Antonio said as he pointed to them.

Moses looked at where Antonio was pointing. "I know where to put two small charges of explosives that will bring down those boulders. I have experience from my mining days with explosives. They should block the river and dam it up. Judging by their size, the landside that they will cause will make a dam about 40 feet high. That should be enough to cause a backflow to change the course of the river back to the south branch."

Rose held up three bags of beads. Moses took two bags. He tossed one to Nick. "I know you know how to place one of the charges on the other side of the river. I will place my bag on this side. You need to place it---" Nick interrupted Moses. "I know, by that loose sandstone below that boulder. Why am I the one that must swim across the river and place that charge? Nick asked. Moses laughed at him and replied, "Because you are younger than me!"

White Elk said, "There's some more things that we will need to do to make this work." Mary said, "Like how are you going to explode the two bags of beads? How do we know the dam will hold, and we are not drowned in the passage below the mountain?" Lo Ming pointed to One Feather and Little Wolf. "It's simple. See that boulder above the passage under the mountain. One Feather will put the last bag of exploding beads under it with the help of Little Wolf. To explode the beads, Mary and June will shoot flaming arrows at the two bags that are under the boulders to explode them. When the boulders dam the river, we will jump in the underground passage and make our way out of this land. One Feather and Little Wolf will shoot flaming arrows at the bag of beads at the boulder above the passage. The explosion should cause a landslide that will take down part of the mountain to cover the passage. We must hope that we get out of way when they blow it. They will have to blow it. We cannot let anyone have a way into this land. That means when we come back for *The Book of Winter*. we will have to fight our way back to the other main entrance."

I watched how everyone had worked it out. Together they were a force. White Elk whispered to me. "Now, I see why you picked them. Together they can solve many difficult problems. I hope that they know it. There are many temptations ahead of them. We cannot lose any one of them. It will take them all to get the book." I nodded, "Let's get this show on the road. There is one thing that June and Mary must do. They will need to time their arrows to land precisely at the same time to bring down the boulders to block the river. If the explosions don't happen at the same time, the boulders won't fall together to form the base of the dam. I once knew a man that would say, "I love it when a good plan comes together."

It took some time for them to get everything in place. Nick swam across the strong current and climbed the steep cliff toward the boulder that Antonio wanted to use to start the landslide to block the river. Several times, Nick slipped and almost fell. When he reached the boulder, he dug a small but deep hole under the sandstone that held the boulder up. Nick made sure there were enough small beads in the opening to start the explosion if hit by a fire-tipped arrow.

Across from Nick was Moses. Moses didn't seem to have that much trouble in getting to his boulder. Moses easily climbed the steep hillside. He took out the bag of exploding beads and buried them in the loose dirt under the boulder. He left some beads out in front of the hole he had dug. By the time he had gotten down from his side, Nick was standing wet on his side of the river. Nick dried himself off with a wet old towel he had from his backpack.

All eyes were on One Feather and Little Wolf. They were having a very hard time getting their bag of beads in place under the boulder they were assigned. There was a small sandstone rock ledge under the boulder. One Feather had to hold out Little Wolf for Little Wolf to be able to place the bag underneath the rock ledge. If One Feather would slip, both of them would fall into the strong current underneath them. They would be swept into the passage underneath the water and probably drown. Everyone held their breath as they very carefully performed their task. It seemed like hours but was only a few minutes until they were done.

It was about noon when all was ready for the plan to be put into effect. Nick had used his mystical skills to build a fire. June had fashioned several tipped arrows that would burn. All the backpacks were packed except for the weapons. I asked Rose to use her crystal ball to see if she could locate anyone on the other side of the mountain. Rose said there were two figures on the other side. An old man and lovely mid-aged woman. The nearest other people were about two miles away. Rose's crystal ball went black. She could get no more good use out of it today. Nick could sense that danger was near. He told everyone to expect a harsh welcome from our enemies when we got out of the passage at the end of the tunnel.

One Feather and Little Wolf moved up the steep side of the hill to be out of the way when they would fire their flaming arrows at the bag above the passage. White Elk said he would light One Feather and Little Wolf's arrows for them. Everyone else was to jump into the passage as soon as the water stopped flowing. They were to run as fast as they could carrying torches that Mary had made

Mary couldn't help it. She went over to Little Wolf. With tears in her eyes, she gave him a big hug. She whispered into his ear, "I love you. I will be back. Be careful, my son." Little

Wolf replied, "Yes, I will mother. Please be careful, I will see you in the Winter season. It our destiny to be together. Now, go mother, you have a job to do!" Mary kissed her son and said, "See you soon."

Lo Ming was chosen to lead. She was the fastest one. Antonio would carry her pack and Nick's pack. Lo Ming had her fighting stick, and Nick had his K-Bar combat knife at the ready. I had my bowie knife and Harken Rifle. Rose said she felt naked without her bags of beads. She took out a white crystal tipped spearhead. Taking a six-foot wooden staff, she placed the tip on one end of the staff. Antonio had his rapier out. Moses had his Australian Brush Knife and whip. June had her tomahawk and bow and arrows. Mary had her bow and arrows ready.

White Elk waved and signaled to Mary and June to light their arrows. When he was sure they were ready, he moved his upstretched right arm down. They both fired their arrows at once. The arrows traveled like missiles toward the bags of beads at each side of the river. Mary fired her arrow a fraction of a second before June's to allow her arrow to reach her target on the far side of the river at the same time as June's.

A loud boom echoed down the river valley as both arrows hit their mark and exploded the bags of beads. At first, the large boulders didn't move an inch. White Elk held up his arms, and a flash of lightning hit the two boulders. The boulders moved a little. Then the loose rock and soil slowly moved underneath them. They both fell straight down into the river below. Other rocks and dirt fell with them. The steep hillsides were covered by smoke and rock dust. The first indication that the dam worked was that the river stopped flowing. In a few moments, the river was down to a trickle. White Elk ordered everyone to jump into the passage and run. We could hear him yelling, "All

I needed to bring down the boulders was a little help from some friends."

We were lucky. The floor of the water passage was solid limestone. We didn't have to run in mud. You could see the light of the passage exit less than a mile away. There was the outline of a man and a dog in the exit.

One Feather and Little Wolf asked White Elk if they should light their arrows. Little Wolf asked White Elk why he didn't use his magic to set off the bag underneath the large boulder above the water passage. "Little Wolf, I can only use so much of my power at once. I don't have enough to do that. Light your arrows and shoot at my signal and not before. We must wait at least ten minutes before exploding the bag. John and the others must have time to reach the other side. If we blow it too soon, they will be buried in the mountain passage. Moses told me that from his mining experience with tunnels, a water passage would probably cave in when the boulder caused the landslide."

We had just gotten to the exit of the tunnel. It had been the Old Man and his dog at the opening. Antonio was the last one out as a loud boom signaled the bag exploding at the other end. Lo Ming pulled Antonio out of the way as the blast caved in the whole passage. Dust and rock blew out of the passage as it closed.

The Old Man and his dog pointed at two figures twenty feet below us. Lo Ming jumped right on top of them. She knocked both down. The rest of us started down the side of the mountain to help her. Moses stopped us. "Let the girl have some fun," he said. We watched as Lo Ming battled the two warriors. Both men had on black body armor and carried long swords. It was good that modern weapons did not work here. This is why the warriors could use and carry medieval weapons.

Lo Ming hit one and knocked him back down. She jumped over the other and hit him on the side of his head. He went down for good. The other warrior jumped up and swung his long sword at her. She hit his sword with her fighting stick. His sword fell to the ground. He took out his small sword and leaped at her, knocking her to the ground. He raised his sword to finish her. As he stabbed at her, Lo Ming's right hand moved in a flash. The man stopped in the middle of his stroke. Lo Ming's dagger was sticking in his right side under his breastplate. He fell dead instantly.

Lo Ming looked at Moses and said, "Thank you for letting me fight them. A warrior must have a fair fight. They died as warriors. I will give them a formal burial." This was not to be. Both warriors turned to dust before our eyes. The old man pointed toward the far forest. Several men in black were running toward us. They were about two miles away. The cloud of debris must have given us away. The old man started to run. He didn't have to say anything. We ran trying to keep up with him.

David didn't move a muscle. He didn't feel any bullets hit him. A long dark snake seemed to fall out of the air in front of him. Its ugly head hissed at him once and was dead on his desk. Donna realized that David thought she was going to kill him. She smiled at him. For once, she had gotten the better of him. "Do you think that I would really kill you. We still need you alive. Believe me, I have thought about it many times. I thought you loved me. How could you marry such a woman as Benita? I thought you had some decent morals left!"

David looked at her. She was as beautiful as he remembered. "How dare you to come here and say such a thing to me? Those many years that I thought you were dead. It about killed me. I loved you with all my heart. We had been working together to save **The Land of the Eagle Feathers**. After you were pronounced legally dead, I went crazy. I felt your grandfather had deceived me. I never heard anything from him in seven years. The Great Elder was supposed to save you. He was supposed to have someone take you back before you were to be killed. That was the deal I struck with him. Explain why I shouldn't have turned on him and the land that I once loved! Explain why you never contacted me," David angrily shouted back at her.

Before Donna said anything more, she noticed something she thought she would never ever see, a tear coming down David's left eye. "My Grandfather, The Great Elder, thought you would never be able to stay here, if you found out I was alive. He thought you might destroy **The Dark Ones** from grief. I agreed with him. It's a pity it took you so long to find out who tried to kill me. Yes, I loved you, once. Now, I don't know. You have become a monster. Word has it that you have taken over many of the other evil empires of the world. You not only killed them, you destroyed them in the most cruel and evil way. It is said that you have come to possess the evil powers of **The Omen.** My Grandfather will never let you back into **The Land of the Eagle Feathers.** The Council believes you have become the same man as your vile father and that you have lost your way."

"There are only two reasons that you are here. One is that you want to kill me, and the other is that you have no choice but to have me help you," David said in a very bitter tone. "You got your one answer. I have not killed you, yet. Like it or not, we have two problems. We have a daughter and a grandson called Little Wolf. They are caught up in this whole mess. I want them to live no matter who wins the final showdown for **The Land of the Eagle Feathers,**" Donna replied.

David picked up the poisonous snake in his hands. As if to make a point, he turned the snake to dust in his hands. "You do have a point. You know that I would never let anyone kill them. You saw that when I helped save John. Now John is another matter. We do not have the say so with John. I think Mary should decide his fate. She is the one who should decide that. Don't you agree?" asked David.

"I agree with you. John should have never been involved with our daughter. He should have known better. We will let destiny take care of him," Donna replied. David could sense some anger in her tone about John. "John is not an easy man to kill. I made the mistake of not finishing him off completely. It was Raven who killed him at the battle. I didn't think the Council would use their powers to bring him back. Is it true that he has only until the New Year to find *The Book of Winter* to save himself?" David asked.

Donna nodded her head. "I always like that you are not who many people think you are. They never saw who you really are, Donna. You have a very tough side. You must have gotten that from your grandfather. If I didn't know better, I would think you want the power contained in *The Book of Winter* for yourself. We are more alike than you think," David said with a smile.

"We were both sent at different times to help defeat **The Dark Ones**. David, you went first. You were chosen because you wanted to redeem you family's name. When my grandfather didn't hear from you, he sent me to find you. I won't go into this farther, but we did find each other. We, like young people, fell in love and had a child. We were going to destroy **The Dark Ones** from within, but things did not go as planned. I only wished things were different," Donna whispered.

Donna could feel it coming back. She had a faint stirring in her heart. David's eyes were betraying his feelings. Eyes don't lie. David stood up and started to move toward her. "Don't David. We are two different people. I don't know if I could ever trust you," she said softly. "That is why we are so much alike. I don't know if I can trust you. Didn't they write in the stars that **The Land of the Eagle Feathers'** fate would lie with two people that once were lovers," David said as he grabbed Donna.

When she felt his touch, she felt her body tremble. David was trembling too. It had been so long since they had felt each other's touch. Both of them wanted more. Perhaps, there could be more, they both knew time was short. Both had had dreams of such of moment. Both had been haunted by them for years.

Donna pushed him back from her. "There is not time for any of that. We must plan for the fate of our daughter and grandson." David replied, "Yes, we need to. I have already set a plan in motion. You will need to convince me as to why I need to save **The Land of the Eagle Feathers**. I have sometimes wondered if the things I remembered about **The Land of the Eagle Feathers** are true. I am beginning to feel that I will need to modify my plans. It will be good to have you back. We always made a good team. We will decide together our fate. We made a blood pack together. We must honor that together. It is our destiny," David whispered in Donna's ear as he pulled her into his arms. Nothing else mattered to him, only her. Destiny had once again brought them together.

Angela had gone back to the safe house that she used to get away from David and his company. Nobody but Antonio and she knew where it was located. As she drove down the dirt road toward a small house in the middle of the woods, she thought about what her next move might be. She would have to get Nick's parents and Shanna to somewhere safer. She worried that someone might see her. She would have to think this through. She had taken great pains in gaining trust with Benita and Raven. They thought she was loyal to them especially since they believed that she killed Donna.

The dirt road ended in a small forest. Angela hid the fact she owned this land by giving the forest to the National Government as a refuge. She had made a stipulation that the government would allow her to live there until she died and not divulge who the owner was. She opened the gate in front of the lovely cottage. She did not mow the grass very often. She wanted to let people think it was abandoned.

She parked her black SUV behind the house so that nobody could see she was there. She went back and locked the gate. She waited a few minutes to see if anyone was following her. As she approached the house, she heard a voice say, "Don't take any more steps until you identify yourself." In the moonlight, Angela could see Nick's grandfather standing in the shadows. "How do you think you would stop me?" Nick's grandfather replied, "With this Eagle Feather." Angela didn't smile back. She recognized the fact that Nick's grandfather had to be a great medicine man. Her father, White Elk, had one just like it. "Let's go inside, we have much to talk about," Angela whispered.

Shanna woke up. A woman was sitting beside her on the large bed. "What are you doing here? Don't you belong in **The Land of the Eagle Feathers**?" Shanna asked. "That's a long story. We can talk about it sometime later. I am glad that you are here. You saved several people that I care for," Donna replied. "Now lie still while I care for you. I made up some medicine that should have you as good as new in a day or so. Drink this cup of liquid and go to sleep. You will feel better by evening. Don't worry, Nick is ok. I wouldn't want to disappoint him. When he sees you next, you better have your strength back. You will need it." Shanna did as she was told. She drank the cup of liquid. It tasted terrible. She said to herself that she had had worse. She fell instantly to sleep.

Wong got to David's office early in the morning. David's secretary asked, "What is wrong with you?" Wong answered, "Don't you see the blood on my shirt. It's David's blood. He had a car accident this morning. David is dead. I must call David's wife and Raven about this. Open his office door now." David's secretary did as she was told.

Wong entered David's office. He locked the door behind him. He moved David's heavy desk a few feet. Pulling back the carpet under the desk, he removed a piece of the wooden floor. Under the floor was a hidden safe where David kept his most secret papers and other objects. Quickly, he put all the items into his briefcase.

He called Raven and Benita again. He told them that he was leaving David's bloody shirt as proof that he had killed David. He had taken David's sports car and put his body in it. He ran it off the road into the deep end of a lake nearby. "Don't worry. I will get lost. I see that you have deposited my money in the offshore bank. David's secretary will spread the news. I will see you in a couple of days." Wong had no intention of keeping that meeting. Instead, he left a note for Raven and Benita. The note was short. It said, "I know you don't like loose ends. Have a Great Day!! Wong." They should get a laugh out of that.

Wong left David's office with the briefcase full. He called the police to say that late last night he saw a red sports car burst into flames and run off the road into a lake. They asked who was calling. Wong said, "I am a concerned citizen." Wong hung up and threw the phone away.

The plan was in full swing. He had put David's wallet and his expensive watch on one of the men that was killed last night into David's car. He drove it to the lake. He wiped his fingerprints clean before driving it into the lake. The man looked somewhat like David. It would be easy for them to think that it was David. He had made sure that it had burst into flames before it fell into the lake. He figured it would take the police at least three days to find the car. Wong went to work like it was just another day. He had given David's secretary the next three days off.

Chapter IX
Everyone is after them:
How will they get back?

The old man and his dog were keeping up a fast pace. June and the others knew this was not the way back to the Eagle Train Station. After about two miles of half running and walking, the old man stopped. It was a good place to stop. They were on a small mountain. From the cliff they stopped at, they would see anyone that could be following them.

Antonio asked the old man, "Where are we going? "Well now, don't you think you have a lot of people after you? Judging by the amount of people crawling around these mountains, you are right popular. If you want to stay alive, I suggest you follow me. There are other ways out of these mountains besides the Eagle Train Station. John and I have already planned on how to get you all out of here safely. Isn't that right, John?" the old man replied.

I looked at the group. We were tired and hungry. "About four miles from here is an old cabin. There will be new clothes and other disguises there for all of us. We will stay there for the night. We will take a short twenty-mile horse ride down to an old abandoned farm. From there, we will split up. There will be transportation available. We will have some lunch and get on down the trail. There is one thing more. Antonio, you will take charge of the group until June, Lo Ming and I meet you at the cabin late tonight. We have some business back down the trail toward the Eagle Train Station. We need to make it look like we are going back to the Eagle Train Station, so they won't be looking for us over here." I informed the group. I could see the group was a little perplexed about who I was taking with me.

The old man told everyone to eat up. He had hidden food by the cliff. There were canned beans, cornbread and other snacks to eat. "Now, Nick, if you could heat up this pot of beans for us and that pot of coffee. It would taste much better," said the old man. Nick went over to the two pots. He placed them between his two hands, and a ball of flame engulfed them. After ten seconds, he cut off the flame. Both of the pots were now boiling hot. The old man was right. The food did taste better hot.

The old man told me that he saw two groups of people about four miles from here back down the trail behind us. While we were eating, Antonio told me he wanted to talk to me privately. We went down the trail to talk. "What's on your mind?" I asked Antonio. "It's Lo Ming. She is more than what meets the eye. You saw how she fought. There is only one person that I ever saw use that move to kill someone. I saw her fight in the colosseum once. It was said that she was related to Fu Hao of China, the greatest general and priest of ancient China. There is a legend that she left the colosseum and started a secret society of assassins. Could Lo Ming be related to her?" asked Antonio.

"I don't know for sure. All I do know is that Lo Ming is considered one of the greatest female fighters in the world. I invited her to come because of her fighting skills and her knowledge of ancient history. Also, she has some type of association with David. That is all I know. Remember, Antonio, keep your friends close and keep your enemies closer," I told him.

"I see what you mean. I wouldn't want Lo Ming after me. I would definitely want to know where she is. Does Moses know about her relationship with David?" asked Antonio. "No, and it is better for him not to know. Maybe, her relationship with Moses will save us from whatever David planned with her," I replied. "We do have one thing going for us. Moses' mother is the only one that is a better fighter than Lo Ming. She knows that she must keep you and I alive to get her husband back." Antonio whistled, "You don't miss much do you, John?"

Nick and the others asked why I chose June and Lo Ming to go back with me. "Well, Antonio and Nick are thinking about getting back to Angela and Shanna so they will be thinking about them. Moses, Rose and Mary are not as fast as Lo Ming and June. The other reason is that the ones I leave behind are good at close fighting. They will be responsible for making sure nothing happens to Antonio. We can't lose him. You will also have to take Lo Ming's and June's pack with you. We will see you after midnight tonight. Don't be surprised to hear some dynamite going off."

I had June and Lo Ming get their weapons. We waved at the others as we headed back down the trail. The old man and his dog were leading the others away to the cabin. When we got close to the place where Lo Ming had killed the two men, we slowed down. After seeing that the other men had went down the trail towards the Eagle Train Station, we followed their trail. After about two miles, we noticed that the men had gotten off the main trail. This had to mean there were others ahead that they didn't want to run into.

We followed the men into the bright autumn forest. The leaves had all turned bright colors. This made tracking harder. The crisp leaves gave off too much noise. We had to be careful not to make too much noise. We located their camp about a mile from the main trail. They had chosen well. There was a small spring for water and several boulders for protection. June silently crawled up and counted twenty men in black with swords and other weapons encamped there. June planted two sticks of dynamite with a long fuse under one of the boulders before coming back to join us.

I told June to light the long fuse at 7:00 pm and run back to the main trail and head back to the cliff. Lo Ming and I would go and find what or whom was further down the main trail. We left June. It was about two hours later that we found the other group down the main trail. It appeared they were from the South American group that gave Antonio so many problems.

This group was very well organized. They had two lookouts near the trail. You could tell they knew their business. Everyone was ready to move in a moment's notice. They did not cook anything on a fire. They were armed with several swords, crossbows and spears. They never talked but used sign language to communicate. They were camped in dense brush so their position could not be seen from the main trail. We moved back from them to talk.

"Are you fast enough to outrun them?" I asked Lo Ming. Lo Ming smiled and nodded. There are two things that you will need to do. First in an hour, we must take out the two lookout guards near the main trail. I will take the one nearest me, and you get the one further down the trail. Then you must get to the main trail and run toward the Eagle Train Station. On my signal, you will light one stick of dynamite and throw it at the camp below. Then, run like the wind to a side trail about a mile down the main trail. That trail circles back to the main trail near where you fought both men this morning. If I am not there, go on to the cliff.

Lo Ming whispered. "That is easy." I told her that there is one final thing she must do. "You must have the two leaders of the group following you. The lead one you must kill and let the other think you are running toward the Eagle Train Station before you jump to the side trail back. That won't be so easy to do." Lo Ming smiled, "That will be no problem. My mother said I was always a little reckless." I told Lo Ming we would start this a little before 7:00 pm. When she heard the dynamite go off from June, she had to have lit her dynamite at the same time.

Lo Ming understood what we were going to do. We would make it look like each group was starting something with the other. If it worked, they would be fighting each other. They would think that the other one started the fight. It would take a while for them to sort it out. That is why we would let one of the two in front live to tell everyone that we had headed back to the Eagle Train Station. This way they would be going toward the Eagle Station as we were going away from it.

The sun was starting to set. The shadows of the mountains were covering the forest below us. I signaled to Lo Ming to move toward the lookout further down the main trail. I moved and crawled toward where my lookout was located. He was on top of a large boulder about twenty feet from the main trail. When I got within twenty feet of him, I took out a short blowgun from my daypack. I put in a dart that was covered with some drug that a chief of an Amazon tribe had given me. When hit with the sharp dart, it would knock out the lookout but not kill him.

I had given Lo Ming the same type of blowgun and dart. Lo Ming knew how to use it. Using blowguns had been part of her martial arts training. I never asked her questions about her past. A Cherokee Chief had taught me the art of using a blowgun long ago. The Cherokee had used blowguns to hunt small game and birds for hundreds of years. I had modified the two blowguns I had to be shorter. It reduced the range. At twenty feet, they would be effective.

I enjoyed watching Lo Ming move toward her target. She moved with the grace of a leopard. She was as silent and deadly as a snake. Whoever taught Lo Ming was a great master martial artist. It was about five minutes till 7:00pm when Lo Ming signaled that she was in position. I signaled her to take out her lookout guard. She and I must have hit our targets at the same time. Both lookouts fell out of their lookouts at the same time. Lo Ming ran back up to the main trail. Lucky for us, the noise of the guards falling was not heard by those below.

Lo Ming took out a match and lit the fuse on a stick of dynamite. She threw it back toward the encampment below. A large explosion could be heard up the trail. June had set off her dynamite. A few seconds later, Lo Ming's dynamite exploded. It didn't take long for some of the group below us to see Lo Ming running down the trail toward the Eagle Train Station. Two men ran up the side of the mountain to intercept her.

Before anyone could realize it, the group that had been by June saw the men from South America. They attacked them thinking they had been attacked by them. The fighting had become fierce between the two groups. After about five minutes, a man came running back to yell at everyone that they had been tricked. The group they wanted had started the fight to get away. They needed to follow him down the mountain toward the Eagle Train Station. It wasn't long before what was left of the two groups ran down the main trail to look for us. I could tell that they were out for blood. Each group had suffered at least ten injured or killed from fighting each other.

When I got back to the meeting place, June and Lo Ming were already there. I would ask them later about how things went. I motioned for them to follow me.

It was about midnight when we arrived at the cabin. Nick had fixed us some supper. We took our time to eat the meal. Mary asked me if we could talk later. I told her in about an hour outside the cabin away from the others. June and Lo Ming told everyone about what we had done. They asked me, "How many were wounded or killed by the fighting?" I told them, "At least 10 on each side. Lo Ming had taken out one herself. This would have reduced the two groups to about ten or eleven warriors each."

The old man and his dog told everyone that they were going. "Now I know it is dark. This is a good time for us to get back to the Eagle Train Station ahead of the two groups. I don't want them to think I had anything to do with the mess tonight. I need to keep a watch on them," the old man said. The old man took his pack and mounted his horse and left down a side trail. You could hear him talking to his old hound dog as they faded into the night.

I told everyone to get some sleep. There were clean bunks with blankets to sleep on. I went out into the night to get some fresh air. It wasn't long before Mary followed me. I told her that there was a small mountain stream near. Nobody could hear us talk over the noise of the stream.

There was a bright moon. Some pioneers and Indians used to call it a Hunter's Moon because you could see so well in it at night. The stream was about 100 yards from the cabin. The moonlight lit up the small rapids of the stream. The water reflected the light making the bubbling water look like a thousand crystals of light. The stream sparkled with the silver light of the moon. The dark mountains behind us made for a beautiful setting. You could feel the magic of the moment. We sat down on some flat rocks near the stream.

"This is a beautiful place," Mary said looking at the stream. "Yes, I know. Some say it's a mystical place," I replied. "We need to talk about us," Mary said as she looked at me. "What do you mean?" I asked her. Mary was beautiful in the moonlight. Moonlight reflected off her soft brown hair. I could get lost in her dark eyes. For a moment, I lost my train of thought. "We have somethings that we need to address," she said. I didn't say anything. She reminded me of that girl I loved several years ago. Her face had changed. Her voice hadn't. I loved her soft voice. It reminded me of the soft wind of the prairie at night blowing through the tall grass.

"I have started to remember some things from my past. I am not totally clear about everything. My father told me that I must find out about my past without any help. There are some visions I recall. I know I am the mother of Little Wolf. I am pretty sure you are his father. I remember when you saw the butterfly tattoo in the spring at the hot springs that you recognized it. Why did you not say anything to me?" Mary said.

"You look so different than when I knew you twelve years ago. Also, I was told you had died in the hospital. I had put some pieces together about things. In some things, I don't know more than you. You are not that young lady that I knew years ago. You are much stronger and harder than that young woman. Likewise, I am not the same man that you knew. I cannot say anything more. You will have to regain your memories yourself. I can say that I never knew David was your father. If I did, things would have probably been different. I did treat Little Wolf like my own son. He is a special young man. Until I heard like you did, I never knew he was my son. The Red Woman has much explaining to do to both of us," I said with an angry tone.

"I don't know about us. Maybe my feelings will change toward you. I am very angry about things. Right now, I have no feelings toward you," she said in a low voice. "Maybe that is what it should be. Fate has always been a strange companion to me. If I don't get my hands on *The Book of Winter*, I will fade and die on the New Year Day of **The Land of the Eagle**

Feathers which is January 15th next year. If you find your memories about me, don't be too hard on me. Please try not to hate me. You must promise me only one thing. No matter what happens to me, you must protect Little Wolf. I don't deserve much more than that," I replied to her.

The thought of John dying was too much for Mary. She realized there were words that she needed to say, "John, I do not hate you. I have feelings for you. During this year, I have grown to know you. You have become a special person for me. The problem is that I don't know who I am. I don't know if you can love me. There are some things that I must work through. I do know that we have a son. Little Wolf comes before either of us."

"But I am a hard woman. I don't know if I can trust anyone. If I find that you played me long ago, I promise I will help you die. You should have known better than fall in love with a young naïve woman," Mary said with a hard tone. Mary looked at me. I could see anger in her face.

"If that is how you feel, and when this is over, you will have my blessing to do just that. I will do one last thing for you. I will help you find yourself, even if it causes us pain. One thing is clear. We don't know how to trust each other. Should we trust each other? I asked. Mary didn't answer because she had no answer. She turned to walk back to the cabin, and I pulled her close to me. She pushed herself away from me. I let her go, but not before I saw the tears running down her face. In the darkness, I watched her silhouette against the sky as she walked back to the cabin. There was no mistake. She was that young woman I fell in love with many years ago. "Yes, fate has always been a strange companion to me," I said to myself. "I just put my fate into the hands of a woman I don't know whether to trust or not."

When I got to the cabin, I saw Mary talking to Rose. Mary and Rose had become very close. I found a bunk. I took off my boots and leaned back. I could hear Mary talking to Rose. They were whispering. I fell asleep. I was too tired to stay awake to listen to their conversation.

"I don't know what to do. I feel betrayed by my mother for not telling me that she was alive. I think she was protecting me and my child. I know my father didn't know that she was alive. He loved her more than life itself. I was little when they told me that she had died in an automobile accident. Her car went off a high bridge in Virginia by the bay. It was carried out to sea in the swift current. They never did find her body. My life has been turned upside down," whispered Mary to Rose.

"I know that it must be very hard for you. I do know one thing. John is very much in love with you. I have watched him. He may not give out much emotion. Watch a man's eyes, they will give his soul away. In a fight, he always moves to your side. He has tried to protect you more than anyone here," Rose said.

"Rose is right. People's eyes give their feelings away. I saw how you comforted him after the Ghost Dance. You won't admit it. Somewhere deep inside, you have some feelings for John. Now, get some sleep. I am tired!" said Lo Ming as she went back to her bunk to join Moses.

We awoke to the smell of fresh coffee, tea and pancakes. Nick had already fixed breakfast. We dressed and ate. Moses had saddled the horses and mules. I told everyone to open the packages on their bunks. I explained to everyone that Antonio would need to get into the museum and out in a hurry. He would have to get the books he needs to decipher *The Book of Fall*. We do not want to let them know that he was already there before Saturday. I feel that he may need to get out of town in a hurry. Everyone would need to be in costume to hide from Kamir's men.

They were to change into the clothes that were in each package. Lo Ming laughed when she saw what was in hers. It was a complete U.S. Army Military Police uniform with shoes. There was a military pistol and belt with holster included. It was tailored to fit her perfectly. Lo Ming wondered how Moses would take it when he saw she looked like a man.

Moses unwrapped the package on his bunk. It contained army fatigues with boots. There were a pair of handcuffs. Lo Ming laughed for the first time in a long time. "I guess you will be my prisoner." We will be handcuffed together. This should be fun. Moses smiled, "I am already your prisoner."

Nick was taken aback when he opened his package. It was a full-dress green uniform of the U.S. Army. It had his unit badges and all the medals he had earned. Antonio whistled at Nick. "I have earned many medals in my life. You seemed to have collected them all. Nobody will ever give you any trouble. If they do, show him this." He tossed a small white box that looked like a tie box to him. "John told me he picked it up in a desert in the Middle East. He said you earned it. Don't take it lightly or you will be insulting those who already have it," said Antonio sternly to Nick.

Rose took the white box from Nick's hands. She opened it. In it was the highest award a serviceman could get. She took it out. It was the Congressional Medal of Honor. "Antonio is right. Never take this award too lightly. It means too much for all those who earned it. Take it home and give it to your grandfather and grandmother to keep. It would make them proud. Then one day give it to your children to remember you by. It is your duty as a father to leave to them," Rose said.

"Thank You, Rose for saying that. I never thought of it that way. My dead friend tried once to tell me that," Nick said with tears. "Yes, I know, he will always be your friend. He came to me one night in my dreams. I told him that you needed to see him," Rose said as she hugged Nick.

I told Nick that wasn't what he will be dressed in. I have another outfit for you to wear. I just wanted you to remember who you are and were. You can't escape from your past. This group needs your skills. At the other end of the bed is a package with your costume," I told him.

Nick went over to the package and tore it open. He found an Orthodox Priest's robe and the rest of the accessories. "There are special pockets for hiding books and other things inside the robes. A man that Antonio knows will meet you at the Houston airport to take you to a special event at the museum in town. Please try not to laugh when you see Antonio's costume," I informed him.

June looked at her bunk. On it was a cowboy hat, blue jeans, cowboy boots and a plaid blouse. "I know that I am supposed to look like a rodeo rider that does barrel riding." There was a blond wig with it. She did like the silver and turquoise necklace that went with it. That explained why the blouse was so low cut. She smiled. "Nothing like hiding in plain sight. They won't be looking at my face."

Rose found a black executive pantsuit on her bunk with a purple blouse. There was a fashionable wrap around white hat with a gold pin to hold it together. Rose was happy that instead of high heels, there were high heeled black leather laced boots with it. There was some jewelry. She liked the gold and pearl necklace.

Mary seemed a little disappointed when she saw what was on her bunk. It was only a black business suit. She did like the fashionable high heels and custom gold jewelry. There was a small handbag with it. She opened the handbag and saw her automatic in it. "I am fine with the accessories."

157

"Mary, you will need to play the part of a grieving daughter. You will need to attend your father's funeral. Don't worry, he is not dead. He is just pretending to be. He was killed in a car wreck yesterday. David said he had to pretend to be dead because Raven and Benita took out a contract on him. Angela will explain that to you later in Houston.

You will need someone to watch over you. Raven and Benita will try to kill you. Don't worry, I will be there. In my package is a black suit. I will be your personal assistant. I will be your driver and secretary. The only people that know me are David and Angela. Nobody there has ever seen me before." Mary replied, "I always wanted a personal assistant. I must warn you that I can be hard on employees if they don't follow my orders."

All eyes were on Antonio. They couldn't wait to see what he was to be dressed as. He looked at the bunk. There was nothing there. "It's in the closet behind you. Take care not to mess it up. It was very hard to get. There are only two of these in existence. A special lady that I once saved from the Germans gave it to me to give to you. Something to remember her by she said," my voice cracked as I told him. Antonio opened the closet door. They gasped at what they saw. It was the most beautiful nun's robe with all its accessories that anyone had ever seen. It was white and trimmed in gold threads. Antonio fell to his knees when he saw it.

"It can't be. She was so special to me. She had told me that I would see her again. She died before I got there. It about killed me. We always joked about things. I loved her with all my heart. I was a Priest then. She was a nun. Some things just are not meant to be," Antonio said choking in emotion.

I put my hand on Antonio's shoulder and said, "Antonio, there is a letter inside the left pocket. She wrote it for you. I never read it. She told me that she had a special place in her heart for you before she died. She also said that she saw your future in a dream. You would be dressed in one of her garments. She said there is one thing she will always treasure: she will have the last laugh. Wear for me, she said, we will be close for one last time."

Antonio got up slowly to his feet. He was pale. His shaking right hand had trouble in removing the old yellow envelop from the concealed left pocket. He could barely walk out the front door. Nobody had ever seen Antonio break down. He was weeping. His heart was breaking. Rose gave him her handkerchief. He made it to the front porch's rocking chair. I shut the door behind him.

The sun was coming up over the mountain ranges to the east. You could hear a flock of geese flying south. The only other things you could hear was a man sobbing as he read a letter written so long ago. A female red cardinal flew and landed in the front window seal. The cardinal watched Antonio read the letter.

We waited about an hour before Antonio returned from the front porch. I had everyone pack their costumes in two boxes to be carried by the mules. I told them that they needed fresh clothes and a good bath or shower. I went behind the stove and pressed a button near the floor. The back wall moved. Behind it was a full bathroom with clothes hung in several dressing rooms. "Welcome to my home away from home. Take your turn in cleaning up. I built this cabin with the back wall touching the mountain behind it to hide this living area. The old man's wife picked out clothes for you. She left your name on each outfit for you. We will leave in two hours. There's plenty of hot water. Nick and Moses will need to help me carry these boxes outside to pack the mules and saddle the horses." The ladies closed the backwall door behind them. They couldn't wait to clean up.

As we carried out the boxes to the outside, Nick and Moses noticed that one was very heavy. I told them to put it down and look inside it. Nick opened the large wooden box and whistled. "What are we going to do? Start a war!" he exclaimed. "Just because, I like my old rifle, doesn't mean I don't know a few things about weapons. To answer your question, Nick, I hope so!"

We mounted our horses in the front of the old cabin. Everyone was clean and fresh from the showers. I asked Moses to lead the mules in back of our line. I asked Antonio in front of the others if he was doing well. "Yes, I am. Don't worry about me. I will wear the nun's outfit with pride. I owe it to her. She once said that I would meet another woman more like me. She said her name would have the word angel in it, but she would not be one. She was right. She was always right. That doesn't make it less painful. We have people waiting for us. Let's get this show on the road. By the way John, where are we going?"

I replied, "We got a shrimp boat to catch. We should be eating catfish, hushpuppies and creole food tonight. By the way, the boat's name is "Rose." The boat's captain is called Big Daddy Crawfish and his first mate is Sheba." Rose said, "Oh, No!"

They were headed to a wide river about 10 miles away. It would be about dark when they would arrive there. The trail that John was taking was about nonexistent. It was very hilly and covered with bushes. Every so often, Nick would jump off his horse and erase the tracks of the horses and mules. He would move fallen limbs and branches of trees behind them to make it look as though nobody had used the trail for years.

After five hours of hard traveling, John motioned to stop. He sent Lo Ming ahead to a small cove that was densely wooded to check to see if the boat was there. He had June go back to see if anyone was following them. An hour later, both of them came back with good news. Lo Ming said that a large boat was in the cove with two people. It had on board a crazy man and a black tall woman. They were grilling and cooking food as if expecting several people for supper. June said as far as she could tell nobody was behind them.

John had everyone lead the horses and mules down the steep trail to the cove. When they got close to the water, John went ahead by himself. John had to admit, Old Big Daddy Crawfish could cook creole food. The old shrimp boat looked like it had seen better days. You would think it was about to sink any minute. John knew that was just a false front. This old boat had a world class engine in it and had outrun many a border patrol boat.

"Old man, where have you been?" yelled Big Daddy Crawfish. "We got a little detained by some old friends of ours," yelled John back. "Stop wastin our time. The food's ready. We'll be eatin in a little bit. Sheba has the grill and soup a goin. Get those youngins of yours aboard. I reckon that means my little girl is with you- all. Her mama wants to see our child. Now get'em here. I'm about starved. If you ruin Sheba's cookin, there a be hell to pay. Now go, you old goat, get um here!"

I went back for the others. Big Daddy was on shore with his john boat. We loaded our supplies into the wooden boat. Big Daddy took Moses and unloaded the boat into his shrimp boat. It wasn't long before we were all aboard. Morning Star appeared from the woods with her horse. She tied the horses and mules together.

Big Daddy asked her to stay for supper. Morning Star said thanks, but it would be dark soon. She had better get the horses down the trail to the local stables. It would take her several hours to get there. Nobody would notice a few more horses and mules in their corral. She would sneak them in late tonight. Sheba went over to Morning Star and gave her a snack lunch to eat. "Nobody goes hungry around me. I toned down the seasoning a bit to match your taste. Now take it, we don't take kindly to people not taken our hospitality," Sheba told her. Morning Star didn't argue with her. She knew better.

Big Daddy Crawfish looked about 60 years old. He is big at about 6 foot tall and wide. He did not have any hair on his head with tattoos on his arms and back. He is a Cajun. Cajuns are mixed blood. I guess he has more races in him than the Kentucky Derby has horses. Now, Sheba was a big very dark beautiful black woman. She has an exotic look. Her dark loose-fitting dress filled with figures, spirits and star symbols made an impression. Her gold and jewels on her necklace accented her lovely dark skin. She looked as if she came from the Caribbean.

"Where's my little girl?" Sheba asked. "I'm here, mama," Rose answered. "Well, look at you. Is that young good lookin man the one that you told me about? He is good lookin. Is he the one that who is goin to help you find your man? If I didn't have a good-lookin man, I'd take him for myself," Sheba teased Nick. "Let's get to it." On the large deck table was a feast. It was loaded with Cajun Food. "There's beer and wine in the cooler. For you that likes good liquor, there's some Tennessee Whiskey and Caribbean Rum over there with fruit juice for the rum," hollered Big Daddy.

For a few hours, we all forgot our troubles. Lo Ming asked Sheba if she was the famous Voodoo Priestess from the swamps of Louisiana. Sheba nodded. Lo Ming said it was an honor to meet you. Mary asked Big Daddy if he was the Wizard of the Bayou. Big Daddy Crawfish smiled as only a Cajun can. "Yes, honey. I'm that and more. Been in the swamps all my livin days. You remind me of someone from a while back. It's your eyes. It will come to me shorty."

They ate and drank until they couldn't anymore. Sheba and Big Daddy put blankets on the deck. It wasn't long before everyone was fast asleep. While they slept, Big Daddy Crawfish started his engine and headed down river in the dark. He knew that they needed to get as far away from here as possible. I wished I hadn't drunk so much good whiskey as I stayed up front to guide Big Daddy around some logs in the river.

It was starting to get daylight. Big Daddy floated his shrimp boat into a small cove. He had figured that they had traveled about 30 miles downriver. When Big Daddy turned off the engine, people started to wake up. It's funny that the lack of noise often wakes people up. Sheba pointed to an old house by the river. We will be going there to freshen up. I will cook everyone some breakfast while you get cleaned up.

"Why are we stopping here?" asked Moses. "This is where we will be splitting up. We will be meeting some people to talk over how to proceed from here. Take the John boat and go to the house to wash up for breakfast. I will be joining you in a short while. I have someone that I will need to see. I will see you all later. Nick and Moses will need to load up our boxes and put them on the porch," I told them.

I went straight to a beat-up pickup truck. I guess it was once brown or maybe it was just that rusty. I opened the driver's side door. "Well, John, it took you long enough to get here," said David. "Don't we make a pair. I don't know whether to kill you now or wait until this is over," I replied. "That makes two of us," I don't trust you either," David answered. I pointed over at a big Oak tree. "You can tell Wong that I am not going to do anything until I get the last book. He can take that sniper rifle off me. By the way, where is Donna and the others?" I asked.

"That's a good question. Nick's grandparents are back in the desert. Shanna and Angela are in the house waiting for Antonio and Nick. It should be a lovely reunion for them," David said with a harsh tone. "Donna is at the Old Eagle Train Station.

"Why is she there? How can she be safe there?" I asked. "Well, I guess it has something to do with the trouble that has been brewing between **Kamir's group** and **The Dark Ones**. It seems that they got into a bad fight between them in the mountains a while ago. I figured you had something to do with that. Raven, Benita and Kamir decided to pull their forces out before anything more happens. Besides, they think you somehow got by them.

I was right. Kamir and them did join forces. My source in my old company says my funeral will be held next Saturday. It's going to be a big deal. The Board of Directors will be coming to it. They will be having a big meeting to decide who will take over my position. Mary, Antonio and Angela will need to be there. Also, Shanna is to get a special recognition for her actions during the last meeting. I assume you told Mary. I also assume that you have *The Book of Fall*," David asked. I nodded "Yes" to both.

"What do you want me to do?" asked David. "I want you to be yourself. I will let you and Donna do your own thing. It is better that I don't know what you have planned. However, there is one thing that you don't know. You will be going to join us in **The Land of the Eagle Feathers.** I need you to take care of someone that can destroy us," I replied. "You mean, my father?" David said in a low voice.

"How will I get back in the land? If I do, they will want to kill me for what they think I have done," asked David. "You better hope you and the Red Woman, Donna, can convince them that you have been working to destroy **The Dark Ones** all the time. If you don't, I won't be the one that kills you," I smiled. "We will see who kills who! Now, take me to the airfield, I have a plane to fly. Stop by that oak tree and get Wong. I do need a bodyguard," David smiled back.

Donna, Red Woman, had gotten on the passenger train back to Eagle Station. It was getting dark. She noticed that she was the only passenger. She expected to be the only passenger. Only a few people ever traveled to Eagle Station. It was starting to rain. It must have been coming down hard to hear it above the rattling and sound of the tracks below. She looked out the window as the train gained altitude. Soon they were above some of the low hanging dark clouds. Every once and a while, a flash of lightning lit up the sky. When that happened, you could see the tops of the dark clouds below.

She leaned back in her seat. The hard, wooden seats were not too comfortable. Her thoughts turned to David. It was hard for her to believe the past few days in Houston. David wasn't the person whom she once knew. Several years ago, they were deep in love. They worked side by side to defeat **The Dark Ones**. They had planned to make sure that **The Land of the Eagle Feathers** would be safe from them. David was her only true love. In some ways, he was the same man but in other ways different. She was not the same either.

David had to feel much the same way about her. She knew that she still loved him. She didn't know if she could trust him. David had to think the same. Why should he should trust her? Twenty years has ways of changing people. She shook those thoughts from her mind. The night of their lovemaking told her different. Whatever would happen, David would never hurt their daughter and grandson and her. What happens to the others could be a different matter.

The lonely whistle of the train reminded her of how lonely her life had been. She had been away from Houston for over 20 years. Her daughter was only 14 years old when she was forced to leave David or die. Raven and Benita had tried to kill her. She was welcomed back into **The Land of the Eagle Feathers** when Angela brought her back and left her. She couldn't believe that Angela had saved her. John later told her that he found Angela at the entrance to the tunnel barely alive.

Angela had faked Donna's death. Donna knew if she ever went back that her daughter Mary would be probably be the next one to be killed. She stayed away for her daughter's sake. When the old man from the Eagle Train Station sent her a message that her daughter was going to have a baby, Donna went back and stole him from the hospital. David made up the story that the baby died in childbirth instead. He didn't know that I had taken him. David said that he hoped that the baby was alright. He was sure that if he didn't cover up the truth, the baby and Mary would be killed. It was the only way to make sure nobody would ever try to find Mary's baby.

Donna felt that Mary must hate her for hiding the baby from her. The rain and thunder were getting louder. The conductor came back. He told her that they would have to stop the train until the storm passed. The engineer couldn't see ahead enough if the rails had washed out. All the lights on the old passenger cabin went out. The conductor told her that it would probably be 30 minutes before they could continue. He needed to go see what was happening and left.

The wind picked up swaying the cabin of the train. Donna thought about the situation she was in. Mary probably hated her. Her husband, David, could never trust her. Who knows what Little Wolf thinks about her?

David had been very loving toward her when she returned. His touch made her feel like a woman again. He always had

166

that magical touch. She could tell that she had the same effect on him. Tears filled her eyes and ran down the dark cheeks of her face as she was torn by so many emotions. Could she trust David? She knew the answer to that. "No," she said to herself. Did she want to trust him? The answer to that was "Yes."

She had raised Little Wolf as only a grandmother could. She was stern but spoiled him. She cared more about Little Wolf than her own daughter and husband. She had mixed feelings about John. Little Wolf was pure and not corrupted by the outside. He was a genius with languages and numbers. He was special. In her heart, she knew that he was the key to getting the final book. Her grandson could be the one that saves the land she loves.

It had been her dream for many years that her daughter and David would return someday to the land. As the wind and rain came down, she knew it was not going to be as wonderful as she had hoped. Her hopes and fears were real. Her love for them was real. She picked up her handkerchief and rubbed her tears away. "Fate was a stranger. Whatever their future was to be was out of her hands. The old train started moving again. The lonely sound of the locomotive's whistle seemed to echo down to the valley below. She had never felt so alone and helpless. Her memories turned to a little girl playing with her father on a bright summer day. They had once been so happy.

Chapter X
What will happen in Houston?
Who is on Whose Side?

I left David and Wong at the old abandoned airport. The runway was still useable. There were two Lear Jets in the old hanger. I watched as David's Jet flew off. David had rented the plane as not to attract attention. Mary's company's jet was waiting for her. Since David's funeral was scheduled only a week away, I would have to change our plans.

When I got back to the old house, I parked the pick-up truck behind a shed out of sight. Nick and Shanna were on the porch talking and kissing. I couldn't blame them. I decided to go around back and enter from the back door. It was no better because what I found was Angela and Antonio doing the same. I excused myself and went into the kitchen. Everyone else was having breakfast.

I asked Moses to go and get the others to join us. We needed to have a meeting. When I had everyone seated around the large kitchen table, I told them there was going to be a change in plans. We had only a week to get the passages deciphered before a Board Meeting of **The Omen** would be held after David's funeral. Mary will still be attending the funeral, but she will have Lo Ming and Moses there. Lo Ming will become her Personal Assistant, and Moses will be her Limo Driver and personal bodyguard.

I tossed Lo Ming a bundle of hundreds. "This will get some suitable clothes for you and Moses when you land at a small airport near Houston. Angela knows the airfield. "What about the pilot of the plane?" asked Lo Ming. "How do you think the company's jet got here? Angela flew it," I replied. She volunteered to fly Mary home from Maine," I replied. "At the airport, there will be the company's long stretch limo with a man that Antonio knows." "Who would that be," asked Antonio. "A friend of both of us who is known as Rico. You are writing his memoirs. He is also a very talented tailor. You will go, and he will dress everyone properly," I answered his question. Antonio looked surprised that I knew Rico.

After going over my plans with everyone, I told them one more thing. Kamir's group has joined **The Omen** and the **Dark Ones**. It seems they thought it didn't pay to fight each other. Raven and Benita must have arranged that. This means that the Board Meeting could be a trap for Mary, Antonio, Angela and Shanna. Don't worry, I will work out how to save you. June, Nick, Moses, Rose, Lo Ming and I will have that covered. There is only one problem. I don't know what David's planning. This should be interesting," I smiled. I knew they had a lot of questions. I sat down and ate Nick's breakfast.

After breakfast, Big Daddy and Sheba sat down on the front porch beside me. "Well, John, we believe you are running out of time. The word in many circles is that you only have until January 15th to live. You should know that there is a huge price on your head and any members of your team dead or alive. We don't know who is behind the bounty. We do know that besides Kamir's group and the **Dark Ones** there is someone else out there interested in what you are doing," said Big Daddy Crawfish.

Sheba had a big frown on her dark face. "There is one thing I should tell you. I have seen Lo Ming somewhere. It appears that she has two sides. She is a talented martial artist. She is a trader in ancient Chinese art. She is one that likes to work both sides of any deal. She is not what she seems to be," Sheba pointed out. "It's funny David said somewhat the same thing. David is one that knows such things. I asked him what he meant. He would only say that she leaves death and destruction wherever she goes. David didn't know if she was working for someone or for herself. He told me to watch her. We will," I replied to Sheba.

"I am worried about Rose. She wants Zan back. That could put her in great danger from Zorn, her ex-boyfriend's father," said Sheba. "Yes, I know. Nick thinks he can help her. There is only one individual that I know that can take care of such an evil man," I replied. "But can you trust him to do it? asked Big Daddy. "David always liked to put people in their place. It

169

takes evil to fight evil sometimes. The David I know would never back away from a challenge. He will do it because his ego wouldn't let him do otherwise," I told them.

"It seems your plans are getting a little too complicated for me," said Big Daddy Crawfish. "Now, Big Daddy, I have known you to have been more devious than me. All you and Sheba will have to do is to be at the Valley of Death by January 13th next year with your crew and friends. I am cooking up a mess of **Dark Ones** for them to play with. The North Pass will be left open for you to enter on January 12th. Don't be late. Take Rose with you to New Orleans. She will need to gather some things for me. Make sure that she gets to Houston by Friday night." I told them.

The last thing we saw of Big Daddy, Sheba and Rose were on the shrimp boat moving off down river. Big Daddy was not letting anyone catch him. That old boat could run. Anyone that does some smuggling has a fast boat. I knew the Coast Guard never could catch him.

I had Moses and Nick load the boxes on Mary's jet plane. They were to take the boxes to Angela's secret home until we needed them. June and I waved goodbye to them. Angela was in the cockpit of the jet with Shanna as her co-pilot. Soon the plane was out of sight. June turned to me and asked, "Where are we going?"

"We are going to take a little horseback ride. We will be visiting Black Panther, White Owl and a tribe lead by Nick's grandfather called **The Others** in the Southwestern Desert," I told her.

"How are we going to do this on horseback? That trip would take a year on horseback!" exclaimed June. "Not on my horses. They are a little faster than most. Let's say they are an interesting breed. A Great Plains Medicine Man gave them to me," I told June. June followed me around to the back of the airplane hangar. Two white horses were eating on a bale of hay. I had already saddled them. "I know the White Stallion is yours. The White Mare must be his mate. Don't tell me, they must be Spirit Horses. They have mystical powers. There are legends about these types of horses. All you have to do is tell them where you are wanting to go, and they will get you there in minutes or hours. Is that true, John?" asked June. "You are about to find out first-hand.

Before you get saddled up, you will need to change your clothes. You are a powerful Medicine Woman. It's time to look the part. There are some clothes in the old office of the hangar for you to change into. White Owl gave them to me to give to you. Now change and get saddled up on the mare and hold on tight. We got a lot of riding to do," I told her.

Mary's company jet landed few hours later at an old closed airport by Houston. A long black stretch limo was waiting for them. Rico was dressed like a driver. Antonio and Nick went up to him. Rico laughed at Antonio. "When John told me that you had been working with him, I knew that the novel you were writing about me was a joke on me," said Rico. "At first, it was. After thinking about it, I let some friends of mine in New York read it. They wanted to publish it. They said something about adult romance was selling big now. They saw a picture of you that I sent. They thought you would be perfect to sell it on talk shows. Several of the women thought you were handsome and mysterious. It's up to you. They should have sent you a check for a few hundred thousand if you sign a contract." Antonio smiled.

"I thought it was a joke until I cashed the check. I guess I will have to become a star. I can't help it if women can't resist me," replied Rico. Lo Ming and Moses walked up to Rico. He took a good look at them. "I have just the clothes that John wanted for you. They should fit perfectly. I will finish them tonight at my place. Angela will bring you by around eight for a fitting. Antonio and Nick will need to change right away. There is a room I set up for them to change in the back of the hangar. I will be taking Antonio and Nick to the museum to get the books he needs. I cannot wait to see Antonio dressed up," said Rico.

"Oh, this must be Shanna's boyfriend, Nick. He is very handsome. I can see what Shanna likes about you. By the way, Shanna, I have that business suit that you ordered with all the special accessories waiting in my limo. Mary, I have heard much about you from my friends about your make-up skills. Let's see if you can make the true feminine side of Antonio come out. There a complete set of make-up items in my limo. Please get them and start working on Antonio. We don't have much time to waste."

It wasn't long before Nick and Antonio appeared from the hangar. Mary had put on Nick a short white beard with gray highlights in his hair. She was able to make Nick look much older. He even had wrinkles on his face. Now, Antonio was a work of art. Without much make-up, she had transformed him into an older woman with just enough highlights in his hair. It was the accents of his eye make-up and the faint shading of his cheeks, combined with some subtle wrinkles that gave him the look of an old nun. Both of their religious costumes fit perfectly.

Angela wanted to hear Antonio talk. She was afraid that his voice might give his disguise away. Angela asked Antonio. "How it felt to be a nun?" "Well, young lady, it makes me feel like a natural woman," he replied. Everyone couldn't believe their ears. He sounded like an old Italian woman. "I can change my voice to sound like anyone, male or female. After all, Shakespeare had to have men play female parts in his day. I must say, I was a hit with the audiences." Antonio said in a sexy female voice. The group didn't know if Antonio was kidding or not.

"By the way, Mary, how did you learn so much about make-up?" asked Rico. Mary answered, "I worked my way through college by doing make-up on people for funeral homes. They said that they looked better than when they were alive. I got summer jobs on Broadway as a make-up artist and on some horror movies." Her answer surprised them especially the part about dead people.

Rico asked Antonio and Nick to get into the limo. "I will tell you what to do by the time we get to the museum. Nick, I know that you can speak some Greek. My sources have told me a lot about you. Make sure you use it, if anyone talks to you at the museum. All you have to do is follow my lead," said Rico. Nick started to say something and thought better of it. The Greek thing wasn't lost on the rest of them. Nick could tell that the others had two questions. How did Nick know other languages and how did Rico find out? It did make sense that John wanted Nick to play the part of a Greek Orthodox Priest.

After Rico left with Antonio and Nick, Angela pulled the jet into a small hangar using a large red four door pickup truck with tinted glass. Let's load our equipment in the back of this pickup truck. We need to get to my hideout to be safe. It wasn't long before they were on the road to Angela's cottage in the woods. Moses said, "Now this is what I call a truck. I always wanted to have one." Angela laughed, "David told me to give it to you if you keep him alive." "Well, Angela that depends," Moses replied. "What does that mean?" asked Angela. "I may have to kill David myself," stated Moses. "I guess you will get this truck one way or the other," Angela laughed.

June saw the dress as soon as she opened the old office door of the hangar. It was white buckskin with sacred precious stones and other decorations covering it. There were white leggings and moccasins. A coup stick was on the office table. A coup stick was used by Indian Plains Tribes for counting coup. This was for famous deeds in battle. The most famous deeds are touching an enemy with the stick and not killing them. June noted that there were two eagle feathers attached to the stick. White Owl must have put them there. This meant that he had chosen two deeds that she had done that deserved the recognition of being the level of counting coup.

June changed into the dress and accessories. There was face paint on the table. Carefully, she put on her face paint. She put a red band of paint around her eyes. Then she put white panther claws into the red paint down into her cheeks. She added some white stars on her cheeks. A head dress of red and gold hawk feathers was on the table. She put the head dress on when she was finished with her face paint. Looking in the mirror on the wall, she was satisfied. Black Panther would think twice when seeing her. He would know right away she was not one to take lightly.

I was waiting by the horses when June walked out of the rusty tin hangar. "You are now who you are destined to be. You are only one of a few. You are a warrior, Medicine Woman and Shaman combined into one. Only the Great Spirits can grant that to you. White Owl must have known this even before you were born. Your parents would have been proud. It is an honor for me to ride with you. May the spirits be with us!" I said as we mounted our Spirit horses. Black Panther had no chance with her. She would convince him, or she would destroy him. It would be his choice.

A voice behind us on a painted pony said, "You have come far, my child. You have far to go. We have been watching you. You control your destiny. May you choose wisely the path you follow." June turned her white mare around to see the young woman on the painted pony. "I feel honored by your words. I will prove that I am worthy of your praise," June replied as she nodded to her with utmost respect. "No, my child, we are honored. May the Spirits of the Stars, Mother Earth, Father Sky, Grandfather Sun and Grandmother Moon be with you," the young woman said as she turned her painted pony into the nearby forest to disappear.

June jumped up on her white mare. I mounted my white stallion. "To Black Panther's camp," was all I needed to say. Both my stallion and June's mare jumped into the air at once. We hung on to our horses as we traveled at light speed. In moments, we were in a dried grass meadow on our horses. Several painted warriors with weapons of lances, bows and arrows and knives were running toward us. We stayed mounted on our horses. A Great War Chief rode up us. It was Black Panther.

I motioned in sign language that we come in peace. Black Panther stopped his horse and took a long look at the young woman beside me. I could see he was impressed. He nodded to her in respect. His eyes were on her coup stick. He had only seen such a woman once before. The young woman before him was a combination of a warrior, Medicine Woman and Shaman.

"John why are you here?" he asked. I pointed to June. June spoke with a voice of respect, "We are here to ask you to join us instead of fighting us. Your tribe's destiny of the future lies in your answer today." "What do you mean?" Black Panther asked. Black Panther's warriors had arrived by now to surround us. They had their lances pointed toward us. "You are known as a wise man. I have come to ask you to consider changing your thoughts. We are like a bird. We need both of our wings to fly together or we will fall from the sky. Without your assistance, we cannot fly and defeat our enemies," June said with respect.

"I fear that nobody can do that for me. Out of respect, I will listen to one that has shown respect for myself and my tribe. Your dress is one of great spirit power. I have heard of your bravery. We are of the same blood and spirit. Come and show us what are your thoughts," said Black Panther.

"I will show you with your permission," said June. "Since you are my guest, we will do as you wish," Black Panther replied. Black Panther motioned for his warriors to follow us. June rode her mare to a steep stone wall behind Black Panther's camp.

June made sure that all of Black Panther's camp had followed us to the stone wall. "Everyone look at the steep rock wall," she said. June pointed her coup stick at the large blank stone face wall. A dark cloud shaded everyone from the sun. June said a couple of words toward the cliff wall. Suddenly, a picture appeared on the cliff wall. "Everyone, please look at that picture. Your future will be shown to you," June said.

The picture of Black Panther's village started to move. His people saw men, women and children being killed and murdered before them. The people doing the killing were dressed in green and black soldier outfits. When everyone was killed, the lead soldier took off her helmet. It was Raven. She laughed at the dead people before her. "That will be your destiny if you do not help **The Keepers of the Yawi** get *The Book of Winter* and keep it from the dark, evil people of the world. These evil people will not only destroy **The Land of the Eagle Feathers**. They will destroy anything good in this world," she said.

June faded the picture into the rock face. Black Panther said, "How do we know that *The Book of Winter* will be used for the good and not for evil?" June pointed to me. "John will be the one keeping *The Book of Winter*. He will be responsible for its use. If he would use it for any other reason, I will kill him with

176

help of **The Keepers of the Yawi**," she stated as she looked at me.

Before Black Panther could say anything, June spoke again. "Black Panther, you are a great chief. You were once a member of the Council. They miss your wise thoughts and great spirit. They miss your tribe. We now must fight as one or all will be lost. You have always had in your heart what is best for your people and what was best for **The Land of the Eagle Feathers**. What do you say?" June held up her coup stick. Everyone saw two eagle feathers on it.

"I must meet with my tribe's council. You can wait at the shade of the Great Spirit tree in the middle of the meadow. You will have our answer before the sun sets in the West," Black Panther said.

June and I walked our horses over to the Spirit Tree. We sat in the shade and watched the birds and other small animals play in the meadow. Black Panther's wife gave us food and drink while we waited.

Black Panther and his council of men and women came back to us. We watch them slowly walk toward us followed by his whole tribe. Black Panther chose his words with care, "We have talked about what you have shown us. We do not make this decision without some misgivings. Everyone agreed to the decision. Your powers are strong. Your voice is true. You will not have to touch your coup stick to us. We will not be your enemy. We have listened to your voice. You have the same voice of your mother's. She was a great Shaman and Medicine Woman. My people and I will follow you."

June nodded at Black Panther and said, "You and your council are wise. The Great Elder welcomes your tribe back to **The Land of the Eagle Feathers**. He feels that you deserve this for protecting your people." June reached into her saddle bag. She gave Black Feather something he never thought he would ever deserve. June reached down and gave him a Golden Eagle Feather. Black Panther held up the Golden Eagle Feather for all to see. His tribe cheered him as only a great warrior would be cheered. "Now go and prepare. You will need to be in The Valley of Death by the first new moon of the season of the cold. May the Spirits be with you," she said.   Then she pointed her coup stick to the sky. Fireworks filled the sky above us. "The Spirits are pleased," she said as our horses disappeared into the sky.

White Owl could feel them coming. The sun was setting in the western sky. The years of being on the plains gave him an appreciation of the wide-open spaces of the west. He often thought of his homeland, The Land of the Eagle Feathers. He missed the green mountains of summer and the mists rising over the valleys in the spring. What he missed most was the thunderstorms that rolled up and down the mountains. The red sky was a warning. He knew what was coming. His tribe had been waiting for years for this moment. It was time to go home.

In the field a few hundred yards away, he saw them riding their magnificent white horses toward him. Yes, he thought, it was time to go home. In the big lodge at the center of their small town, he had called a tribal meeting. It would start at sundown. He had told his tribe that a very special person would be coming. He had watched everyone going into the lodge from this hilltop. The pictures and paintings on the walls of the lodge would tell everyone it was time to go home.

John and June stopped their horses in front of White Owl. June noticed right away that White Owl had on his best ceremonial dress. June was still in her ceremonial dress with her headdress and face paint. John didn't say a word. White Owl mounted his mustang and motioned them to follow him. He would be taking them to the meeting lodge.

Everyone in the tribe had been summoned to attend the meeting. This included members that worked in nearby towns. The lodge had a ramp for horses to enter the big arena used for different events. John, knowing what would be happening, decided to remain outside the lodge. This meeting was for tribe members only. John respected that tradition. Even though the tribe had always treated him like a member and respected him, he still felt a little like an outsider.   This was just one of those things he had learned to accept through his wanderings over many years. This was June's moment not his. He would only be a distraction.

White Owl entered the arena on his spotted, tan and brown mustang. The members of the tribe stood to watch them enter in silence. When June entered in her ceremonial dress with her headdress and face paint, a gasp could be heard echoing through the building. There was disbelief in what they saw. For many years, a large painting had pictures of different scenes from the tribe's history. The last scene on the mural was a young woman in a white dress in a headdress with a painted face carrying a coup stick with two eagle feathers on a white Spirit horse. This was the moment that they had been waiting for. Everyone knew it was time to go home where they belonged.

June knew there would be some doubters about her. She would have to demonstrate that she was the real thing. When she reached the center of the large arena, she turned her horse to face the crowd. White Owl rode his mustang to the far end of the arena. He knew it was up to her to convince them.

June took a hawk feather from her headdress. She threw it into the air. The feather became a large brown hawk and flew around the arena. She took a golden hawk feather from her headdress and threw it up into the air. That feather became a large golden hawk. She held out her arms, and both hawks landed one on each arm. She put her arms together, and the hawks disappeared and in her hands were two hawk feathers. She put the hawk feathers back into her headdress. She reached around and took out a large golden eagle feather. She threw this golden feather into the air. The golden feather became the largest golden eagle that anyone had ever seen. Its wingspan was over twenty feet. The golden eagle flew around the arena. Each time, the eagle flapped its wings, precious stones and gold dust fell into the crowd below it. June got off her white horse. She whispered into its right ear. The white horse flew up to join the eagle. They flew together out of the arena and disappeared into the night.

A large clap of thunder shook the building. In the middle of the arena appeared the vision of the Great Elder. "Greeting from **The Land of the Eagle Feathers**. This is the day that we will start fulfilling the destiny of our tribes and land. We know that you left **The Land of the Eagle Feathers** to protect your tribe's children. It is with deep regret that you felt shame in doing so. You should not feel that way. My vision is here tonight to tell you to come home. We need you. Let us become one people again. The final battle to save our sacred land is upon us.

As you can see, the final chapter of **The Land of the Eagle Feathers** is upon us. We will either live together or die together. That is our destiny. This world is not your place. You belong in the land of your forefathers and mothers. We belong together. When **The Keepers of the Yawi** find the final book of seasons, we will be protected from the evil forces forever. There is one more battle to fight in the Valley of Death. You are great warriors with a spirit and heart that we have missed. We will welcome you with open arms. You must decide if you want to join us again. It is time for you to come home. Only you can decide if you want to make that sacrifice.

We will understand whatever you decide." The vision of the Great Elder faded into the air.

June spoke to the members of the tribe. "You know me. Many of you knew my mother and father. They fought for our ancestral land and died. You have a chance to save our ancestral land. Your destiny calls you. We have the chance to become one again. Some of our blood may be spilled in that Valley again. To die a warrior's death is a death with honor. It is your decision to make. I will await your answer at the sacred ground on the hilltop. May the Great Spirits be with us." June took her coup stick and waved it seven times above her head. A flash lit up the arena. June was gone.

The Great Elder of the tribe called the meeting to order. "This decision must have every members' approval, or we will remain here. If you approve, please stand and hold up your hands. If you do not, please remain seated." White Owl and the tribe's Great Elder observed what the tribe's fate would be.

June sat in the middle of the sacred ground. She waited for word from the tribe. The late fall sky was full of stars and planets. The air was cold. It will frost soon. Winter will be approaching from the North to cover this land in white. A figure approached her. It was her Grandfather, the Great Medicine Man of the tribe. He sat down beside her. "You have come far, my child. The tribe has spoken. On the new moon of the winter's season, we will be joining you in the Valley of Death. It is our fate and destiny to be there. May the spirits be kind to you," he told her. He took her into his arms. She felt like that little girl again in her grandfather's arms. A tear fell from his cheek. He didn't have to tell her that he loved her. She could feel it in his arms.

The sound of two horses' hooves striking the rocky ground broke the silence. John didn't have to say a word. June got up and bid goodbye to her grandfather. Her grandfather watched as they rode out of sight. He was worried not so much for June. It was John. Destiny has a fate all its own. John's destiny was always one controlled by outside forces. He had always beaten the odds. This time might be different. The Great Medicine Man looked at the stars. It will be wonderful to be back home again. That was his destiny. In the sky above, two shooting stars shone bright in the sky. A smaller one followed the larger two. The old Medicine Man felt joy for the first time in a long time. It was a sign that one day he just might become a great grandfather. Destiny only knows if that will come to pass. If he has anything to do with it, it will.

It was late evening when they arrived at the sacred cave of **The Others**. Nick's grandfather and grandmother had called a council meeting of their tribe. **The Others** had left **The Land of the Eagle Feathers** long ago. They had decided to make their home in the desert of the Southwest. It was their destiny to live in the desert but not to forget their tribe's ancestry.

Whenever **The Land of the Eagle Feathers** was in trouble, their warriors would go back and fight to save it. It was their duty. The members of the tribe could go and stay in the land at any time. Some of the members of **The Others** would do so. There had been some concern within the tribe that they were losing their tribe's spirit. Many of its members had taken jobs in the city instead of living in the desert.

Nick's grandfather had just started the council meeting in the sacred cave. Torches were lit all around the cave's interior. He signaled to the other council members to be silent. At that moment, June walked into the cave. One of the council members pointed to a painting on a cave wall. The painting matched June perfectly.

June nodded toward the council as a sign of respect. She knew that she did not have to prove herself to anyone here. "You know why I am here. Your Medicine Man and Woman has already told you I would be arriving. I come to ask for your help. **The Land of the Eagle Feathers** needs your assistance one last time. This will be our last battle to save it. You are great warriors. We respect your customs and spirit. There will be one final battle at the Valley of Death. It will be for survival of the land. It will be for *The Book of Winter*. This book is the only way that we will be forever free of the evil forces that attack us. However, this will also be the last time that any of you will be allowed back into The Land of the Eagle Feathers. If you want to stay there, you are welcome. We understand if you want to return here. We know that many of your tribe feel that this world has corrupted you and your families. There are those of you that may want to stay in the desert. It is your home. We only ask for assistance one last time. We will understand whatever choice your tribe members make. The Great Elder wants me to bless your tribe. He has a gift to give you for your many sacrifices over the years."

June took her coup stick and waved it over her head eleven times. There were eleven members on the tribe's council. They were seated around a large marble table. As June finished her eleventh wave of her coup stick, a golden eagle feather appeared on the table in front of them.

Nick's grandfather said, "We thank the Great Elder for his precious gift. It is our duty to protect our ancestral home. Unless a member of our council objects, we will come. We will tell our members that this is the last and only time they will be able to go back to the land and stay. I will come because of two reasons. First will be to save the land. The other reason will be to try to save our friend, John. There is not a member of the council here that has not been saved in battle by him. We owe him that much respect. Those that want to come will be at the Valley of Death on the first moon of the winter season. I will be there." said Nick's grandfather, the Great Medicine Man of the tribe. All the council members stood up. "We will come for both reasons. Warriors are warriors until the end. Warriors respect warriors until they die in battle together," they chanted together.

Rico drove Antonio and Nick to the Houston Museum. There was a special exhibit on religious artifacts open to the Museum's donors and honored quests. Rico parked the limo on the front street in the VIP parking space. A line of donors was waiting for them. Rico was a little worried that Antonio and Nick wouldn't be able to answer their questions or pull off the deception.

A gentleman in a gray suit asked Nick in Greek about whether he had visited several sights in Rome. Nick replied in his best Greek that he had had only time to visit four of the sights. Nick quickly turned the conversation over to a different subject on Greek history. Rico was impressed with Nick's Greek knowledge and accent. Nick asked the man if he could talk in any other languages. The man said, "I do talk Italian and English." Nick replied, "As they say, in Rome do as Romans do. Since we are in America, speak American English." The man agreed by speaking in English.

Antonio was busy answering several questions about the Catholic Church's policies on various subjects. Having just came from the Vatican a few months ago, he easily answered their questions. Luckily, Rico interceded and told everyone that he had some new religious artifacts that he had put in this office just for the guest priest and nun to see. He told the audience that he would have them back shortly. "Enjoy the refreshments. We have made many types of samples of food from various countries and drink as much wine from those countries as well. There is coffee and tea for the rest of us. Us Italians would take offense if you don't indulge yourselves," Rico greeted his guests.

Antonio noted several people both men and women that he knew. The ones that he was worried about belonged to Kamir's group. He wondered why they hadn't bothered him and Nick. Perhaps, they wanted him to get the books before they kidnapped him. It he was lucky, Kamir's group may have bought their act. Antonio couldn't be sure. It would be better if they use plan B to get out of the museum.

Rico took them back to his office. "Here are the texts that you requested, Antonio," said Rico as he pointed at the desk in his office. "I would be an idiot if I didn't know what they are for. You are going to translate *The Book of Fall* from **The Land of the Eagle Feathers.** Aren't you? That is the last book that tells where *The Book of Winter* is at in the land. There are many that would give their lives to find that book. No wonder, Kamir's men are here," pointed out Rico.

Antonio and Nick did not say anything. They stuffed the old texts into their costumes. "We will be using plan B to get out of here, Rico. John has already rewarded you for your service. In this note, there is the location to a valuable work of art that is centuries old. Do what we need done, and you can have it. If you don't, my people will blow you and the art up," Antonio stated bluntly. "Have I ever crossed you? Rico asked. "Yes, remember Paris several years ago?" replied Antonio. "That was just a misunderstanding between friends!" Rico tried to explain.

Nick took two smoke bombs from under his garment. He gave one to Rico. "I will throw mine down the hall into the stairwell. You will throw yours near the back of entrance going to the hallway to your main exhibit. On the count of twenty after you throw the smoke bomb, pull the fire alarm and run out yelling "Fire." That should cause enough confusion for us to get away. Don't double-cross us or Shanna and Angela will visit you sometime!" stated Nick. "As much as I would like a visit from those two lovely ladies, I would not look forward to them coming," replied Rico.

The plan worked out better than they thought. Rico pulled his alarm as told. The smoke bomb in the stairwell made it look like the fire was burning several floors above. In the confusion, Nick and Antonio ran out a side entrance and jumped into a black, window tinted van that was waiting for them. Lo Ming was driving with Moses in the passenger seat. "Did you get the painting, Moses?" asked Antonio. Moses said, "Yes. Who would ever expect an old, bent over man with a cane taking it?" The robbery will give Antonio cover for helping us. It will also guarantee that Rico can be trusted. That's his favorite painting. He will want it back," laughed Antonio. Nick looked worried. Kamir's group was waiting for us. Someone must have told them," said Nick.

Angela was seated in the back seat. "I cannot lie. I did it. For David's plan to get rid of Kamir, I needed to show that Kamir couldn't be trusted." Antonio wasn't too happy about being blindsided by Angela not telling him. "If I did, my love, you would have not probably gone through with it. You would have been too nervous to put on such a good show. You are kind of cute in that Habit of yours. Don't worry, I will make up for it tonight," Angela whispered in a sexy voice that everyone could hear. Lo Ming smiled a wicked smile as she drove skillfully dodging traffic. Lo Ming thought as the others thought, "Now that's my kind of woman."

After they got back to Angela's cottage, Antonio said that he could not wait to get this costume off. Naturally, Angela told him he could go to her bedroom to change under one condition. She would need to help him get the habit off. She didn't want to see him mess up the habit. "I will make sure that you don't tear or mess it up." Antonio turned red in the face, but he didn't object to her offer.

Mary turned on the television to watch the local news. The local media was covering the robbery at the museum. It appeared that everyone was buying that the smoke bombs were part of a robbery plot. One thing was clear. Rico really missed his favorite painting. He was crying when he talked to the news reporter about his painting being stolen on television. "If I didn't know better, I think Rico thinks he will get some sympathy from his women friends tonight," said Mary.

Nick wanted to change his clothes. Shanna took Nick to the basement to change. There was a shower and an old bed that she was using to sleep in. "I can't wait for you to get out of these clothes and take a good shower. I am much better now than the last time you saw me. I just want to show you how much I love you. After all, your magic words saved my life. Now, what were those words again?" asked Shanna. "I think it was something like this, I love you," Nick said as he took Shanna in his arms.

There wasn't much to do until Friday night. The Dark Ones' Council meeting had been postponed until after the "Wake" at David's house. In David's will, he had instructed that everyone should be at his house with his coffin in the large main room. There would be plenty of food, fine wine and the best liquor for everyone. They would have a viewing of his body at midnight. That would be the ending of the "Wake." Mary was to invite everyone including Kamir. His will made special mention that even his enemies should have a good drink on him. It also said that anyone that was invited would receive an expensive token for coming.

Antonio set up a study in the small shed outside the cottage to decipher *The Book of Fall.* He soon discovered that the passages were very easy for him to decipher. He could do it with little or no help from the texts he got from the museum. The first passage he deciphered was for himself.

Your Mind Lies

You see with your own eyes
My brother and sister, the mind lies
You must look beyond you
 To know what is really true

You hear with your own ears
What you hear may be your own fears
You must listen to another voice
To know what is the right choice

You feel with your own soul
What you feel you may not know
You must feel with another's heart
To know which place to start

You think with your own mind
What you think may be blind
You must think about what others say
To know what is the right way

You must think, feel and see like another
To find the right way, my brother
You must see with another's eyes
My brother and sister, your mind lies

The next one he deciphered was for Lo Ming.

Everything is a Part of the All

There is no joy without pain
There is no growth without rain
There is no false without true
There is no me without you

There is no hate without love
There is no below without above
There is no courage without fear
There is no far without near

There is no death without birth
There is no sky without earth
There is no day without night
There is no wrong without right

There is no low without high
There is no star without sky
There is no weak without bold
There is no warm with cold

Everything is a part of the reason
Everything is a part of the season
The answer will come with a birth of a fawn
The day is darkest just before the dawn

The darkness will give way the day
The deer will come out to play
The crow will let out a call
Remember everything is a part of the all

This one was for Moses.

The Mountain Loves Only the Sky

The misty fog makes love to the mountain
The lonesome frog waits in the fountain
The river is destined to cry
The mountain loves only the sky

The river makes a mournful sound
There is no other river around
It doesn't even try to pretend
Its tears are carried in the wind

The wind will tell you why
The river is destined to cry
It may not speak or shout
You hear it at the river's mouth

Where the river kisses the land
You find a way to understand
You will a way to know
The answer is in the river's flow

The sky will make love to the mountain
The tears of the river will flow to the fountain
You will know which way to go
Hey, Yi, Hey, Yi, Hey, Yi, Yo

This one was for Mary.

What Happened to Me

Who's that looking back at me
Who's that person that I see
It's someone I don't know
Where did that other person go

I don't know that person with dark hair
Who's that person standing there
I have never seen this person before
It doesn't look like me anymore

Who am I looking at today
She doesn't look like I did yesterday
Someone's taken my place
What happened to my face

Why do I see pain in her eyes
Maybe it's the mirror that lies
Surely this can't be true
What happened to the girl I knew

There's someone I don't know
Where did the other person go
Who's that person that I see
I don't know what happened to me

He liked the one that was for Nick.

All the Parts Make a Whole

Be as strong as brother bear
Fierce in battle but always fair
Hunting in the shadows of the night
Looking for food, not wanting to fight

Be as faithful as brother wolf
Beautiful to see but fleet in foot
Howling at its lover in yonder moon
Missing its love, gone too soon

Be as wise as brother owl
Hidden to most but above the bough
Watching in the tree always watching you
Telling you he knows what you do

Be as gentle as brother deer
Harmless to all but living in fear
Hoping they won't be someone's prey
Trying to survive for another day

Learn from the animals that you see
They are all brothers to you and me
Each one has a soul
All the parts make a whole

The next one surprised Antonio, it was for David.

There's a Bad Storm Coming

There's a bad storm coming
Ain't no use in running
No matter how you try
Can't get away from Father Sky

There's a bad storm coming
Ain't no use in running
No matter where you hide
Can't get away from what's inside

There's a bad storm coming
Ain't no use in running
No matter who you know
Can't get away from the river's flow

There's a bad storm coming
Ain't no use in running
No matter what you do
Can't get away from you

When you hear the thunder's roar
You can't run and hide anymore
There's a bad storm coming
Ain't no use in running

The next one was for June.

Like a Bird With a Broken Wing

Without my tears, I can't cry
Without my wings, I can't fly
Without my voice, I can't sing
I am like a bird with a broken wing

Haunted by love that didn't last
Tortured by sins of the past
Bitten by snakes the devil sends
Betrayed by love that only pretends

A garden cannot grow without the rain
You can't know joy without the pain
A day cannot exist without the night
You can't know wrong without the right

It is time to make a choice
It is time to listen to your voice
It is time to stop trying to hide
It is time to face what's inside

Nothing is right if everything is left
It is time for the healer to heal thyself
You have a voice and you can sing
You don't have to be a bird with a broken wing

Rose would like hers'.

Listen to Each Bird's Song

Every bird greets the morn
When a new day is born
Every bird sings its song
They are where they belong

You hear in the song of the sparrow
I know which way you should go
Following the trails of the deer
You will find a place that's clear

You hear in the song of the chickadee
I can see what you need to see
Look for the tree that glows at night
Then you know to turn right

You hear in the song of the red bird
I hear what you already heard
Remember what's been taught to you
Then you will know what to do

Remember east is west, west is east
Best is worst, worst is best
Wrong is right, right is wrong
Listen to each bird's song

The next to last one was for Little Wolf.

A Child of Destiny

Every season has a reason
Every reason has a season
It is and will always be
You are a child of destiny

It takes every minute to make an hour
It takes every petal to make a flower
It takes every rock to make a mountain
It takes every drop to make a fountain

The flowers and trees need sunlight to grow
The rivers and streams need rain to flow
Without the rain, the land cannot give
Without the land, the people cannot live

You are a child of this land
Even though you don't understand
There's something you're destined to do
It all starts and ends with you

You come from the land of the brave
You'll find your answers in a cave
It is written in the North Star's glow
It is hidden in the rivers flow

Little one, don't you cry
Listen and learn, don't ask why
Every reason has its season
Every season has its reason

The final one is for John.

One of a Kind

In the memories of yonder days
Time visits but never stays
Visions of ancestors dance in the mind
Living in the day but looking behind

Seasons change as seasons always do
Skies of gray, skies of blue
The river never ceases to flow
Grass will die, grass will grow

Mother Earth has wisdom we don't understand
The answers are hidden in this sacred land
Open your eyes and try to see
The way it is and will always be

Father sky will give you the light
Grandmother moon will give you the night
Mother Earth will give you the dirt
Grandfather sun will give you the earth

You must look beyond yourself
Look to your right, look to your left
Look forward, and then look behind
You will see the white buffalo, one of a kind

When Antonio finished his task, he looked at what he had written. There were two passages that bothered him. The one that was for him, and other one was the one for John. His passage reminded him that everyone had their own reasons for being here. He couldn't even trust himself. Why not possess the powerful **Book of Winter** for himself and Angela? There was a warning in that passage. He was not the only one that might want the book. He started worrying that the closer they got to finding the book, the more tempting the power of the book would be. He remembered the saying, "Once a scorpion, always a scorpion."

John's passage gave him insight what was going to happen to John. Antonio had grown fond of John. John was like him in some ways. John, like him, had wandered this earth for many years. It had been his destiny. Fate has its way of choosing your destiny. He had seen how the Great Elders and others had looked at John as if they knew something about his fate. Antonio watched as the dry wind of autumn blew across the Texas grasslands. The waving grass reminded him of waves of the oceans. "Only time will tell what shores each of us will land on," Antonio thought. "Soon everyone would be here for David's Wake. This should be fun. We only will have to survive it."

Chapter XI
The Wake:
How will everything change?

It was a stormy night as the quests started to arrive at David's mansion for his Wake. Lightning flashed and lit up the mansion and the surrounding gardens. Large twisted Oak trees lined the long driveway up to the old gray stone mansion. If one's residence was any indication of one's soul, the twisted trees and old English style gray stone mansion would describe David's soul. Mary was at the front door to greet each quest as her quests got out of furnished black limos.

Mary was very gracious as she welcomed each one. Lo Ming dressed in a lovely oriental red silk evening gown with black dragons embroidered on it with precious white pearls directed everyone to the main room. Lo Ming smiled to herself. The guests couldn't help but look at her beautiful gown with a long slit that showed off her long legs. Moses was assisting Lo Ming. He was dressed in a black tux. Moses didn't wear a bowtie. He left it off, and Lo Ming had him open his shirt to show off his muscular chest. Lo Ming thought that would give guests something to look at besides her. Well each to their taste she thought.

There was a small band playing soft music. Tables were loaded with food of every description. Several waiters and waitresses handed out drinks of all types. Rose dressed in a flowing red low-cut gown that showed off her best assets. She handed each guest a satin bag with June's help. June was dressed in a stunning golden gown. Each of the bags contained gems and precious stones and some gold nuggets fashioned into a long gold chain. The male guests got diamond cufflinks in their red bags, and the women got diamond earrings in their black bags.

The final guests arrived. Antonio was with Angela followed by Nick and Shanna. They both made lovely couples in their formal attire.

In **The Land of the Eagle Feathers,** Little Wolf became worried for his mother. The moon had a red blood color this night. He knew what that meant. His mother and **The Keepers of the Yawi** were in danger. He knew that Mary, his mother, was faraway in another land at a place called Houston. Before his mother and the others left The Land of the Eagle Feathers,

Antonio had told him that he felt that things in Houston might go wrong for them. Antonio told Little Wolf that he needed Little Wolf's help in case Antonio didn't make it back. In the evenings when everyone had been asleep, Antonio had met with Little Wolf. They had both worked on *The Book of Fall* together in secret. Antonio was very pleased with Little Wolf. Little Wolf was a genius with language. Little Wolf could decipher the pages of *The Book of Fall* without any help.

Antonio told him to keep it a secret from everyone. The last night before leaving Antonio handed several copies of pages to Little Wolf. Antonio told Little Wolf to finish deciphering these passages and to give it to anyone that makes it back. This way, if anyone steals the book from him or he gets killed, they will be able to find *The Book of Winter*. Antonio also said one last thing, "If the moon turns blood red, Little Wolf, you must say a prayer to the Great Creator. It will help to save us from danger. It is written in the last page of *The Book of Fall* that to save all a little wolf must howl his prayer to the Great Spirits above as the blood moon makes its descent." Little Wolf asked Antonio, "Why are you telling me this? I have heard that you are not to be trusted." Antonio replied, "Because like your mother and father, I have a son here also."

The Wake was reaching its high point. At midnight, the invited guests were thanked for coming and asked to leave. The final part of the Wake was to begin shortly. The guests were told to keep their gifts. Lo Ming and Moses escorted them out to their awaiting limos to leave.

After everyone had left, Lo Ming and Moses went back into the main hall to signal to Mary that the final part of the Wake could start. In the center of the main hall was a very long oak conference table. Mary asked that The Board members of the Dark Ones called **The Omen** be seated around the table. When everyone was seated, Mary told them that the final part of the Wake would begin.

In the back of the room were two people dressed in hooded robes. One was dressed in a black robe, and the other was dressed in a red robe. Mary got up and welcomed both as guests to the final part. She motioned to Antonio to come forward toward the conference table. Antonio did as he was told. Antonio came forward to talk.

"I have been to **The Land of the Eagle Feathers** several times this year. I am making my last trip soon. I know that **The Omen** wants the land for themselves. You want the riches of the land. However, there is one thing that all of you would want more than the land's riches. Everyone here knows the legend of the four books of **The Land of the Eagle Feathers** is the greatest prize of all. David and Angela came to me last year. They asked me to find these books to lead them to the last of the four books, *The Book of Winter*. To say that the feat of finding the first three books was difficult would be an understatement. There were many that wanted the books for themselves or didn't want anyone to have the power that they contained. We had to fight both to get the first three books."

Antonio had a gem covered brown book in his hands. "This is *The Book of Fall*. It has the location of the final book in it, *The Book of Winter*. I have also been working for the Chairman of the Board to find that book," Antonio stated. The Chairman nodded to Antonio. People started whispering to each other about what had been said by Antonio.

The Chairman of the Board stood up and motioned to the person in the red robe to come forward. "You can uncover yourself now," he said. The person uncovered his hooded robe. It was Kamir. "Welcome, Kamir, I am glad that you have come. We have some unfinished business with you," the chairman said. Before the Chairman could speak, the person in the black robe came forward.

All eyes were on the person in the black hooded robe. The person came near the front table. The person motioned to the Chairman to sit down. As the person uncovered their hood, everyone including Kamir gasped. The person in the black robe was none other than David. There was total silence in the large room.

David took his time to carefully look at everyone present before he spoke. He looked at Raven and Benita. Raven had a scorn on her face. She was not pleased that David was alive. Benita was another story. Her face started turning red. Then, a face of fear showed on her face. "Benita, my lovely wife, and Raven, my supervisor, my death has been greatly overstated. I am very glad to see you attending my Wake. Please forgive me for this deception! I had to find out who was betraying me. I knew about Kamir. There was only one person that would have been able to allow Kamir to get into the last meeting of the Council. I now have proof. Mr. Chairman, why did you let Kamir in? said David.

The Chairman stated, "Because if anyone had gotten their hands on *The Book of Winter,* they would be more powerful than me. I knew you were getting close to obtaining the books. I did not want anyone to be more powerful. I figured that I would not be safe. Besides, it was just business, it was not personal, David?" David laughed at the Chairman as he pointed his finger toward the Chairman. "It was to me!" as a bolt of lightning hit the Chairman. The Chairman was dead. That meant David would take his place. It was the law of the jungle. If you were powerful enough to take out the Chairman, you could take over his position. David enjoyed himself for a few moments. He looked at Raven. She wasn't taking it too well. Now, David was her boss. She would have to report to

David. Benita seemed confused. David was her husband. She didn't need to have an alliance with Raven anymore. She would have all the benefits and powers that she always wanted being David's wife. She smiled at David. It was one of those smiles that meant, you don't have to worry about me anymore. I need to see that you live. I won't come after you. Benita grabbed Raven's leg under the table. Raven understood what Benita wanted her to do. Raven was to be quiet.

The other members of the Council stared at David. This situation had turned everything upside down. They knew the rules. He who is the strongest leads. To have that much power to defeat the former Chairman would easily be able to defeat the Council. They knew that David must have been collecting power and waiting for his chance to take over. It really didn't matter to them as long as David didn't attack them. They would still get their cut of the bonus money. They would sit back and watch for a while.

In **The Land of the Eagle Feathers**, Little Wolf did as Antonio said for him to do. Little Feather looked at the blood red moon and started his Prayer to the Great Creator and Spirits.

Great Creator, Mother Earth and Father Sky

Looking below, looking high
Mother Earth, Father Sky
Looking left, looking right
Great Creator of day and night

The lonely wolf howls at night
He sees his lost lover in the moonlight
The hungry bear digs at the root
Listening to the sounds of ancient flute

The mighty buffalo hunts for grass
He longs for the glory of the past
The skinny squirrel climbs the tree
Looking for acorns that cease to be

The starving deer walks in the snow
He looks for food that ceases to grow
Sleeping bears dream in their den
Waiting for a new season to begin

We ask you to understand
We are brothers and sisters to this land
We ask you to hear our cry
Great Creator, Mother Earth and Father Sky

Kamir was startled at what was happening. David had just taken over the Chairmanship of The Omen. David looked at him with his utmost disrespect. Kamir knew his time was numbered. It would do little good to say he didn't try to kill David. David wouldn't believe him anyway. "I know it was you who tried to kill Antonio. You knew I needed him to complete my plan to obtain the book. Kamir, too bad you weren't any smarter, I could have used you for my plans," said David with distain in his voice.

Kamir knew his time was short. He had to try something to stay alive. He had a couple of cards to play before he was going to die. Kamir jumped over the table and stood behind Mary. He held a knife to her throat, "You can't kill me. I will kill your daughter if you try. Besides, you invited me to your house. You know the rules. If you invite someone, you can't kill them in your home. I guess the board and chairman wasn't invited. They just assumed. They made a big mistake by coming without a formal invitation.

"Yes, Kamir, I can't kill you here, but she can. She didn't invite you here," as he pointed to Lo Ming. "She is not powerful enough to do that," laughed Kamir. "Again, Kamir, you underestimate your enemies," David said. Lo Ming had a golden spear in her hands. Kamir looked at it in fear. It was the only thing that could kill him. "Yes, that is the Sacred Spear of the Amazon Great Spirits, Kamir. I took it out of the safe several days ago. Don't you remember, Lo Ming? She does have more power than you. "Yes, I do. She is very powerful. Kamir looked at Lo Ming in disgust saying, "How could someone as powerful as you lower yourself to work with David?"

Kamir saw that look in Lo Ming's face that meant he would not get an answer to that question. Kamir thought that at least he would do something that David would couldn't stop. He would kill David's daughter. Lo Ming saw the slightest movement of Kamir's hand. In response, Lo Ming threw the spear as Kamir started to cut Mary's throat. Lo Ming thought she would be too late to save Mary. Much to everyone's surprise Mary vanished before the spear hit Kamir in the heart.

Little Wolf felt someone beside him. Mary stood there beside him. She took him into her arms. The Great Creator and Spirits had heard his prayer. They had protected his mother and transported her to him to save her. Mary whispered to Little Wolf, "How did you do that? "Antonio told me to save you. There is a price. You must promise to protect One Feather and June." Mary nodded her head. "That was Antonio alright. He always had another reason to do good," she smiled. As they say, "Once a scorpion, always a scorpion," she thought.

David was confused by what had happened. The same was for everyone except Antonio. David didn't know where Mary was. He believed that Mary must be safe. He carefully examined everyone's face. The only one that didn't look surprised was

Antonio. He could feel that Antonio was the one responsible for saving Mary. It didn't matter right this minute. He had other things to do.

"As the new Chairman of the Board, these are my orders. I have made a blood pact with the leader of the group that is going to get *The Book of Winter.* I will be going with them to **The Land of the Eagle Feathers**. Benita, being my wife, will be in charge of **The Dark Ones** while I am gone." Benita couldn't believe her ears. David was making her number two in the organization. This was too good to be true.

"Antonio has deciphered *The Book of Fall.* David asked, "What does it say?" said David. Antonio looked at the Council, Raven and Benita. "The book states that to find the last book. A group consisting of the following must work together: **The Keepers of the Yawi** which includes Mary, your daughter, Angela, and Shanna, the others I will keep to myself. For some reason, the book states that the leader of the most powerful enemy of **The Land of the Eagle Feathers** must accompany the group. I presume that will be David. It states that David and his followers will have one last chance to obtain *The Book of Winter* if the book is found.

In the Valley of Death, there is to be a great battle between the two groups on January 15th of the New Year. Both groups will be allowed to enter the land from a tunnel in the mountains. You know where the Valley of Death is. That is where the last battle was fought. The winner of the battle will get *The Book of Winter* to use as they wish and all the treasures of the land. There are only two stipulations: only three hundred members of each of the groups will be allowed to participate in the battle with non- gunpower type weapons, and that each leader and representatives sign a blood pact that they will abide by the rules. If anyone should not follow that agreement, they will be destroyed. So is the destiny of those that win that this must be followed stated the book."

"How would that happen? How would one get killed by an agreement?" asked Raven. "Each of you will be signing the Document called, The Oath of Soloman. As many of you know, by signing that Oath, the document will send emissaries to kill each of you that violates the agreement. Nobody has ever signed The Oath of Soloman and violated the agreement and lived. This has been true for over hundreds or thousands of years," answered Antonio.

"Where is this document?" asked Benita. A man from the back of the room walked toward the table. He had on an off-white cavalry hat with a faded seven on its side. Everyone at the table had heard of this man but had never seen him until now. One member of the board said out loud in a soft voice, "This is the one called John. They say he is half ghost and half alive. We have never defeated him in battle. I heard he is weaker now since the last battle about 12 years ago."

John walked over to the conference table. He put his hand into the inside coat pocket of his leather jacket and pulled out a rattlesnake. He put the rattlesnake on the table. The members of the board started to move away. John told them to stay where they were seated, or the snake would bite them. The rattlesnake hissed two times and turned into a golden document of paper. "I will sign the document first, and David will sign it last. This pen is very sharp. It will draw blood from one of your fingers by placing it on one of your fingers. You will then sign the document with it. It will be a blood oath. You know what that means," said John.

"We have all our people here. Where are your people?" said Benita. "They are all here around you. The guards and the service people are my people." Benita and Raven looked around. There were many people standing around them lined up. "Don't get any ideas of doing anything, young lady. You wouldn't stand a chance with all of us. Why even Black Panther is here? Just sign and get this over with. My wife and I got better things to do," said Big Crawdaddy.

It took over an hour for everyone to sign. David was the last one to sign. "Now all of you get out of here. My wife and I have some celebrating to do," David said to everyone. "We have only a week before I go to the land. Benita will be in charge while I am gone. To make sure that you don't try anything with her, I put in a small sentence in the agreement that you promise to keep her safe." Benita put her arm around her husband and smiled.

David told Benita to help escort the guests out. While Benita was doing that, David turned around to see where I was. "How did you know that I would be able to persuade everyone to sign the oath? What would you have done if they had refused, John?" David asked. I looked at David and told him that I had that covered. I pointed to a dark area at the top of the stairs in the back of the big room. I motioned for Nick to come out of the shadows. In Nick's hands was a M60 machine gun. I pointed to another corner in the of the upper stairway. I motioned for Shanna to come out into the light. She had a 308-cal. sniper rifle with a spotting scope.

"I told them if things go wrong to take out everyone except you. We need you. The only surprise that I had was Lo Ming. How did you and Lo Ming know each other?" I asked David. "That's a long story. She didn't know me directly until we met going after you. Many years ago, her grandmother did some work for me. She was killed by Kamir and his men after she found the Spear of the Amazon for me. Kamir found out that they had found it. He wanted to get it to keep himself safe. When she told him that she had sold it to me, he killed her grandmother to keep anyone else from knowing where it was.

You know me. If I can kill two things with one stone, I will do that. It worked out for me. There is one thing that I will tell you. Lo Ming is more than she shows you and me. She will hunt down every one of Kamir's followers and kill them. That is her reputation on the dark web. It appears nobody knows who she is. Oh, by the way, I could feel Nick and Shanna on the upper stairs. I knew you needed me, so I knew I was safe for now." David replied with a wicked laugh.

"For now, you are. Be on that train to the Eagle Station in a week at midnight!" I told him. I pointed to the lights. The lights slowly dimmed to complete darkness. It took a minute or two before the lights came back on for David to see what had happened. David looked around. John and all of his people were gone. "Well, I see that John has learned more things than I thought. When this is over, we will have one hell of a fight. Too bad, I wish things could have been different. Destiny does have a way of its own," David thought to himself. David knew why John didn't just kill everyone. The book set the rules. Also, John could destroy the rest of the **Dark Ones** by destroying the **Dark Ones Army**.

The week passed quickly. Shanna and Nick went to see Nick's grandparents. Antonio spent his time with Angela at her cottage. Mary went to Maine to see her friends. Rose decided to visit a friend in New Orleans. June went to spend some time with her tribe on the plains. There was only one problem that I had. Where did Lo Ming and Moses go? I had an idea. They left a note for me. It said that they will be at the Eagle Train Station when we got there. They had some loose ends to tie up.

It was a cold night. They night was dark due to no moon. The old train engine blew out some steam that blocked our view of the mountain above us. Everyone was on board except for Lo Ming and Moses. Nick, Shanna, Rose, Antonio, June, Mary, Angela and David. David had been the last one to board the train. The old conductor yelled, "All aboard." David sat with Mary. They seemed to be discussing something.

The conductor told everyone that Moses and Lo Ming had been on the train a week ago. They were already at the Eagle Train Station. I could see that most of them were wondering why they came so early. David looked at me. I knew he guessed why as well as me. David went over to me and said, "Loose ends. Lo Ming doesn't leave loose ends."

The old train clanked and moaned up the steep grade. It would be about three or four before we would get there. The old man must be expecting us. I could see the lights of the Eagle Train Station from here out my window. I kind of missed him and the old hound dog. It would be nice to see him once more.

The train slowed as we came into the station. The old lanterns lit the way. The conductor unloaded our gear on to the boarding flatform. We picked up our gear and headed into the station building. I could sense that something was wrong right away. The old man and his dog should have been waiting outside the station building for us.

As we entered the station building, we saw the old man with his dog seated in his old rocking chair. His arm was in a sling. He had a bandage on his head. He looked at us. "Well, I have some good and bad news," he said. "Well, old man, give us the good news," said Antonio. 'The good news is that Kamir's followers are up the trail," said the old man. "What's good about that?" asked Nick. "Lo Ming and Moses are after them. Knowing Lo Ming and Moses, they will be taking care of them. I don't know about their leader. I am glad to see David. He can take care of him," answered the old man. "What do you mean that David can take care of their leader," asked Mary. Before the old man could answer, David said, "Because he is my father!" I looked at the old man and asked, "What is the bad news?" The old man looked at us and said, "We have a much greater problem than that!"

Rose says, "I know the answer to that. I saw it in my cards. Antonio, where is **The Book of Fall**?" Antonio opened his pack. His face told everyone the answer. **"It's gone. The book is gone. This is a book of blank pages!"** The old man looked at everyone carefully, "Which one of you took it? Every one of you have a reason?" I know that you all know the legend of **The Book of Fall**. There is a map in it of where a buried treasure is hidden somewhere on this side of the mountain range. It was put there on purpose to get people to stop looking for **The Book of Winter**. Isn't that right, David?" David nodded his head. "I will ask the question one more time. Who took the book? Remember your lives depend on having that book!"

Before anyone could answer that question, the old wooden front doors to the station slowly creaked open. Two people were standing there. A storm had been brewing outside. A flash of lightning hit a tree behind them. This flash lit up the two figures. The two figures were their comrades: Lo Ming and Moses. Their clothes were covered with mud and red blood. They had a wild look in their eyes. Lo Ming had a bloody silver spear in her hands. Moses had his large bush knife dripping with fresh blood in his.

The old man looked at Lo Ming in fear. His old hound dog beside him stood up and growled at them. The old man started to say something. A clap of thunder shook the building with dust falling from the ceiling

Lo Ming had that look in her eyes of a predator that had found its prey. Everyone had seen that look on Moses' face before, and it wasn't good. As if in slow motion, Lo Ming and Moses lifted their weapons at the same time. Lo Ming and Moses threw their weapons.

Lo Ming's silver spear hit the old man in his chest. The bush knife did the same to the old hound dog. They both fell to the dusty floor. A smile formed on Lo Ming's face. Antonio yelled, "Lo Ming! Why?" Another large clap of thunder shook the old station. All the lanterns blew out at once followed by a flash of blinding lightning. Complete darkness filled the room. Lightning hit another tree outside lighting up the room for a spilt second. Lo Ming and Moses were gone. Nobody dared to move. They could hear the two old front doors closing in the darkness as the storm raged.

About the Authors:

Joe G. Morin was born and raised on a small rural southern Indiana farm. He currently lives in East Tennessee where he taught Adult Education for several years. His ancestors came from France, Scotland and Ireland. His current publications on Amazon.com are *Why Men Have Problems with Women and An Angel in the Kitchen.*   He loves to tell stories. He is from a family of story tellers. He would listen to his Grandfather tell his stories about being a rural schoolteacher and farmer for hours. You may contact him at joegmorin@gmail.com

Jo Ann Bullard was born in East Tennessee. Having been a professional entertainer, she traveled all over the world. There is no place like East Tennessee. She lives and writes in the foothills of the Smoky Mountains. Her ancestors were Cherokee, Blackfoot and Scotch-Irish. Her current publications on Amazon.com are *The Problems with Men, and An Angel in the Kitchen.*   She has written several articles for professional publications.   She is currently working on a volume of song lyrics. You may visit her at ja2bullard@gmail.com

This Book is part of the series about The Quest of the Land of the Eagle Feathers.

This is the third book in a four-part series.

The first two books are:

The Quest of The Land of the Eagle Feathers:
The Book of Spring

The Quest of The Land of the Eagle Feathers:
The Book of Summer